Christmas Riches

H.L Day

Other books by H.L Day

Too Far series
A Dance too Far (Too Far #1)
A Step too Far (Too Far #2)
Temporary Series
A Temporary Situation (Temporary; Tristan and Dom #1)
A Christmas Situation (Temporary; Tristan and Dom #1.5)
Temporary Insanity (Temporary; Paul and Indy #1)
Fight for Survival series
Refuge (Fight for Survival #1)
Standalones
Time for a Change
Kept in the Dark
Taking Love's Lead
Edge of Living
Short story
The Second Act

Copyright

Cover Art by H.L Day
Edited by Alyson Roy - Royal Editing Services
Proofreading by Judy Zweifel at Judy's Proofreading
http://www.judysproofreading.com[1]
Christmas Riches © 2019 H.L Day

. . ⚓ . .

. . ⚓ . .

Christmas Riches is a work of fiction. Names, characters, places, and incidents either are the product of the author's imagination or are used fictitiously, and any resemblance to actual persons, living or dead, business establishments, events, or locales is entirely coincidental.

. . ⚓ . .

Warning

Intended for an 18+ audience. This book contains material that may be offensive to some and is intended for a mature, adult audience. It contains graphic language, explicit sexual content, and adult situations.

---

1. http://www.judysproofreading.com/

THANKS

Huge thanks to my beta readers Barbara, Tan, and Sherry.

Blurb

Opposites might attract. But does that include age?

Christmas comes early for Aiden Malone in the form of a seductive, blue-eyed stranger down on his knees. But a shocking revelation about his new "friend" has him running for the hills and cursing his stupidity before the night is out.

Tom's not prepared to give up that easily. He may be rich where Aiden's poor. Innocent in a way that Aiden isn't. And on the wrong side of twenty. But he's old enough to know what he wants. And that's Aiden. He just needs to persuade the older man to look past his hang-ups about age and wealth.

Lust and prejudice pull Aiden in opposite directions, severely testing his willpower. As Tom's layers begin to peel away, Aiden discovers the younger man's life of privilege may not be all it seems. If Aiden gives in, they could have the sweetest Christmas that either of them has ever tasted.

But Tom's about to shatter their joy with a surprise announcement. Decisions need to be made on both sides. It's down to Aiden, though, to stay strong and decide whose happiness is more important. His? Or Tom's? Because they can't have it both ways.

It's possible their relationship won't even last as long as it takes for the snow to melt.

Chapter One

I tipped my head back against the partition wall, desperately trying to ignore the low hum of voices from outside the bathroom stall that reminded me where I was. That and the faint strains of Elton John singing "Step into Christmas." I didn't really want to be thinking about Elton John at a time like this. Glancing down, I bit my lip in an effort to hold back the groan that threatened to escape. It was difficult to know what was hotter, the sight or the feel of what the stranger was doing. As if sensing my scrutiny, pretty blue eyes the color of sapphires rose to meet mine as he pulled his mouth off my dick. Fully erect, my cock waved in the air, glistening obscenely from the man's saliva. My eyes pleaded with him not to stop. I would have used words but they seemed to have escaped me somewhere around the time his lips had opened wide to take me in.

He appeared completely unfazed by the fact that he was crouching on a bathroom floor as his gaze trailed down my body, his voice a husky whisper. "Undo your shirt. I want to see your chest while I suck you."

Fingers trembling with arousal, I hastened to do as he asked, the desire to come blanking everything else from my mind and making me momentarily forget that at thirty-one years old, this was not what Aiden Malone did. Especially when The Royal Oak wasn't even a pick-up joint. It was an ordinary run-of-the-mill pub in Battersea, just down the road from the building site where I worked. Families came here on the weekend. They even held a goddamn quiz night there every Thursday, along with the occasional karaoke on a Friday. It was about as far from a pick-up joint as you could get. Yet, when my eyes had lingered for that little bit too long on the man walking toward the exit, he'd hesitated, his path changing course to saunter in my direction.

I'd averted my gaze, embarrassed to be caught checking him out so openly, fastening it instead on a garish Christmas decoration dangling from the pub ceiling, its gold metallic covering reflecting the light as it twisted in the breeze. It hadn't deterred him in the slightest, and within seconds, he'd been standing right in front of me. I don't know what I'd expected him to do, offer his name maybe, or ask for my number. He'd done neither. The stranger had given me a thorough once-over, his gaze taking in my dark hair, prone to curling especially when the weather was damp, my grey eyes that a boyfriend had once said were the color of a stormy sky, and my stubble because I hadn't bothered to shave that day. The gleam in his eyes said he liked what he saw. He bent over so that his lips were close to my ear, his warm breath ghosting over my skin and raising goosebumps. "I want to suck your cock. Come with me." Then he'd held his hand out, like it was that simple.

I'd stared at him, the invitation leaving me breathless, unable to tear my gaze away from his plump, pink lips. Lips he'd just offered to wrap around my cock. I'd imagined in vivid detail what it might feel like to push my cock between them and feel his tongue explore the length of my shaft. My hesitation had lasted just that one beat too long. With a small shrug, he'd started to retreat, the fingers inching back, the invitation in the process of being rescinded just as quickly as it had been offered in the first place.

He'd been seconds away from turning and leaving and I'd known I'd never see him again. He'd be just a faint, amusing memory of something that could have been. Triggered by a strange sense of panic, my hand had jerked out, grasping on to his fingers before he could withdraw them completely.

The seductive smile I'd received in return had been everything. He'd pulled me to my feet, our fingers still entwined, and I'd followed blindly without having a clue where we were going. I'd almost balked when I'd realized his destination. I wasn't a "bathroom sex" type of guy. I'd been in relationships where boyfriends I'd trusted implicitly had suggested it with a wink and I'd always declined, pointing out that we weren't teenagers and we had homes to go to. Why choose to get it on in a place like that when there were other options available? I'd never understood it. Not before, anyway.

The blue-eyed stranger had led me into a stall, ignoring the interested stare of the middle-aged guy at the sink washing his hands. Slamming the door shut and pushing me back against the side of the stall, he'd wasted no time in dropping to his knees on the floor that appeared relatively clean. But who knew? His long-fingered hands made short work of the button and zipper of my jeans before pulling my semi-hard cock out. He'd regarded it with a look of intense fascination, his tongue coming out to taste before he'd slid the length between his lips.

And there we were.

I undid the last button on my shirt and placed my hands against the wall behind him, not knowing what else to do with them. He smoothed his fingers along my thighs before parting the two sides of my shirt as if he was unwrapping a very special Christmas present, his gaze hungry as he devoured the sight he'd uncovered. I didn't go to the gym. I didn't need to. I spent eight hours a day, five days a week, carrying heavy loads of bricks around, digging and clearing, and anything else manual you could name that needed doing on a building site. The honed muscles therefore came naturally. He slid his hands over my six-pack, kneeling up to continue his exploration all the way to my pectorals, his fingers tweaking my nipples before he sank back down, his lips engulfing my cock again and bringing a strangled gasp to my lips. He certainly knew what he was doing.

Voices grew louder outside the door before fading away again. I had no idea how long we'd been in the stall. It felt like hours and mere minutes all at the same time. He tilted his head, the angle allowing him to take me deeper. My thighs trembled, the first tingles of orgasm starting to make themselves known. I was ready to come, but at the same time it felt so damn good, I wanted it to last a bit longer. I lifted my hands from the wall, digging my fingernails into my palms to create enough pain to prevent me from coming for a few more delicious seconds. A few more seconds where I could enjoy the hot velvet warmth of his mouth and the feel of his talented tongue on my cock. It probably wasn't fair. Not when his jaw had to be aching by now, but at the moment, selfish felt way better than fair.

I gave in to the temptation I'd had ever since he'd started blowing me, my fingers sliding into his thick, dark hair, the strands soft and free of any hair products. I was hesitant at first. When he didn't pull back or complain, I slid them deeper, my palm cupping his delicate skull, encouraging him to tilt his head farther back, my cock nudging the back of his throat. And he took it perfectly with not an ounce of protest. When the blue-eyed stranger's hand moved to palm my balls, there was suddenly no pain in the world sufficient enough to keep me from coming.

Sparks raced down the length of my spine, my whole body tingling as the rush of orgasm coursed through me, my muscles spasming and twitching as if someone had applied an electric shock. They gradually died away, replaced by a warm lassitude that started at my crotch and radiated outward. Eyes closed, I rested back against the wall, panting, dimly aware that I should be concerned about how much noise we'd made. Or I'd made. But I couldn't bring myself to care when the warm, talented mouth of a complete stranger had just taken me straight to heaven, and I wanted to stay there a while longer. Besides, it wasn't like there was anybody banging on the door and threatening violence. I took that as a good sign.

Sensing movement, I opened my eyes to find myself facing the amused scrutiny of my stall companion head-on. At some point while I'd been lost in post-orgasmic lassitude, he'd stood, putting us back on the same level. He moved closer. *Was he expecting me to return the favor?* He might be comfortable kneeling on a bathroom floor but I wasn't.

The blue-eyed stranger leaned in, his hand bracing against the wall by my head. I waited, still struggling with the dilemma of what I was supposed to do. "If you come home with me, you can fuck me."

I stared at him, the words slowly unraveling themselves in my brain to form a sentence. That hadn't been what I'd expected him to say.

Not at all.

Apparently reading my stunned expression as reluctance, he spun around, unzipping his jeans and lowering them a few inches, along with his underwear, to reveal a decidedly pert ass. As adverts went, it did the trick. A smirk playing on his lips, he glanced back over his shoulder. "What do you think? Interested?"

I nodded; my gaze—and brain—was still fixated on his ass. I may have only just come but my dick didn't seem to be getting the memo. My dick, I realized, that was still hanging out. I reached across the stall, grabbing some toilet roll from the dispenser and giving myself a quick wipe before tucking myself back in and sorting out my clothes. The buttons on my shirt seemed to take much longer to fasten than they had to undo, the stranger's eyes on me just as much as they had been when I'd undressed.

When I was decent, we left the stall together—the bathroom blessedly empty. No one batted an eyelid as we made our way through the pub lounge, Elton John having given way to Mariah Carey. Either the patrons hadn't realized what we'd been up to, or they just didn't give a damn. As we passed the table where I'd been seated earlier, I eyed the pint of beer I'd barely touched. It was destined to stay that way now. I had something far more interesting to do.

We tumbled out onto the street, the cold, frosty December air causing an involuntary shiver to wrack my body. My companion hailed a black cab and I followed him into the back of it. It dawned on me that I hadn't uttered a single word since this weird interlude began. It was time to change that. I glanced over at my companion. The man who'd already blown me, swallowed my cum, and who I was going to fuck. The man whose name I didn't even know. Nor had he asked for mine. Was this how things were done these days? Was I that far out of the casual-sex loop that all the rules had changed and I hadn't even realized it? The blue-eyed stranger's head was turned away from me, his gaze focused on the passing scenery outside the car window.

I cleared my throat. "I don't even know your name."

His gaze flitted in my direction before returning back to where it had started. "You can speak. I was beginning to wonder."

I waited, doubt slowly starting to creep in, its insidious fingers wrapping themselves around my brain. *What the hell was I doing?* I hadn't bothered to listen when he'd given instructions to the driver so I didn't have a clue where he'd told him to take us. I could ask him. But if he wasn't even willing to volunteer his name, then it was doubtful he was going to repeat information he'd already given, just because I wasn't listening. At the moment, we were still in Battersea, the streets comfortingly familiar. The sensible thing to do would be to get the driver to stop while I could still walk home. I opened my mouth, ready to tell him to do exactly that when the man next to me spoke first.

"Tom. My name's Tom. What's yours?"

I relaxed slightly, thoughts of telling the cab to stop drifting away under the strange, comforting blanket of a name. "Aiden."

"Pleased to meet you, Aiden. I'd shake your hand but I think we've already gone past that point."

Heat crept up my cheeks and I was grateful for the gloom in the back of the cab. I wanted to ask him if he did this a lot and what had made him come over and speak to me. Well, apart from the fact that I'd been broadcasting my interest to the entire pub. But with the name exchange done, Tom had returned to his vigil at the window, so I stayed silent, using the cover of darkness and the fact that his attention was focused elsewhere to study him.

He was younger than I was. If I had to guess, I'd have put him somewhere in his mid-twenties, which was a good five to six years younger than I was. I'd dated guys who were a couple of years younger but nothing beyond that. But then, this wasn't a date, was it? It was... I wasn't sure of the current vernacular. A hook-up?

I continued my inventory. Black jeans, a red T-shirt depicting some sort of band I'd never heard of. At least I assumed they were a band. I couldn't think what else they could be. He had a slim build like a gymnast—a marked contrast to my own bulky muscles. Tom hadn't seemed to mind though. In fact, the way his fingers had traced the muscles of my abs almost reverently had screamed that muscles were his thing. An expensive-looking leather jacket topped off his outfit.

My gaze drifted upward—clean shaven, sharp cheekbones and of course those gorgeous lips. My dick twitched at the memory of them wrapped around it. Would he do that again when we got to wherever we were going? Maybe if I asked nicely. I wondered what his cock was like, the anticipation of getting to find out making me shift restlessly in my seat. Dragging my mind away from sex, I took in the last few details on display that I hadn't already catalogued. Very little jewelry, a watch and one studded earring in his left ear that looked like a diamond, but was more likely to be some cheap imitation.

Resigned to there being no further conversation between the two of us, I pulled my phone out, finding a text from one of my closest friends and workmates.

JT: *Thought you might be down at the pub, mate? Was going to join you for one.*

Tapping out a quick response, I relaxed back into the seat and closed my eyes. It wasn't until the cab lurched to a halt that I opened them again. I sat up straight, squinting at the house we'd pulled up in front of and wondering if there'd been some sort of mistake. "Where are we?"

Tom glanced up from where he was paying the driver. "Richmond."

Richmond. Home of the wealthy. "And you live here?"

He nodded, already reaching for the handle to open the cab door.

I turned my attention back to the house. To say it was huge would be an understatement. There had to be at least ten bedrooms in a house that size. It was set away from the street at the end of a long driveway, the entrance blocked by a sturdy wrought iron gate, the security system flashing its warning from a distance. The place reeked of money. A house this size in an area this affluent couldn't have cost anything less than five million pounds. How the hell did someone in their twenties get to live in a place like this? Had he inherited it? Or was he some sort of business genius who'd made it big at a young age? The man in question was already out of the cab. He leaned back in. "Are you coming?"

That was an excellent question. *Was I?* The house had thrown me for a loop and I wasn't sure I wanted to set foot inside it. I barely had enough money at the end of the week to afford food. Whereas if Tom lived here, my monthly rent was spare change to him. We were worlds apart. *What was I... his bit of rough? His walk on the wild side?*

A polite cough from the cab driver forced me into making a decision. I'd come this far so it seemed churlish to refuse to get out just because Tom was rich. I joined him by the gate, Tom radiating impatience. He'd already deactivated the security code and had the gate held open. I stepped through, waiting a few moments while he closed it. Then I followed him down the driveway, the gravel crunching loudly beneath our feet. Just like in the cab, Tom remained silent. It seemed like my blow job companion—and soon-to-be fuck partner—wasn't much of a talker. We came to a halt in front of a large, ornate front door, a huge Christmas wreath covering almost the top half. Tom pulled a key out of his pocket and unlocked it before ushering me inside.

My gaze flitted around as I tried to take in as many details about the house as I could, starting with the entrance hall where we were currently standing. It was decorated in neutral tones, a few paintings the only thing to break up the bare expanse of wall. The carpet was deep and plush, my feet sinking into the luxurious pile. It was the sort of carpet that made you feel guilty when you realized, as I did now, that you were still wearing shoes. Tom hadn't asked me to remove them though, so I had to assume it was okay. The entrance hall was dominated by a curved staircase, its carved mahogany balustrade leading to the rooms upstairs. Above my head, there was an honest-to-God chandelier, like the ones I'd only ever seen in stately homes or on the TV before.

All the doors leading off from the entrance hall were closed, apart from one. I made an effort to peer into the murky gloom, but the only thing I could make out was a huge Christmas tree. It was clear from everything I'd seen that this house was way out of my league. It would follow, then, that Tom was too.

If he'd been aware of my wide-eyed stare as I took in my surroundings, he was too polite to mention it. He inclined his head toward the staircase. "Let's go straight upstairs."

Chapter Two

The room Tom led me into was just as opulent, if not more so, than the entrance hall had been. It didn't take a furnishing expert to work out that everything from the four-poster bed to the thick velvet curtains was of the highest quality.

Something, apart from the cost of the decor, bothered me about the room but I couldn't quite put my finger on what it was. I watched as Tom played about with a dimmer switch, making tiny adjustments until he was satisfied with the amount of light in the room. He shrugged his jacket off, draping it over a chair close to the window before turning back to look at me. "You seem like you're about to run away."

"Do I?" It was easy to see where he'd gotten that idea. After walking through the door, I'd barely taken two steps inside. "I don't normally do this sort of thing."

His head tilted to one side and he regarded me as if I was a new species of exotic animal which had been discovered in the middle of the jungle. "What sort of thing? Blow jobs in the bathroom? Or going home with someone you've just met?"

I swallowed thickly. "Both of those things. I probably sound stupid admitting that, but it's true."

His eyes softened. It was only at that point that I registered the perpetual air of cynicism he'd worn up to that point. Even while sucking my cock, it had been there in the almost arrogant tilt of his eyebrow and the self-assured way he'd gone about it. An almost smile hovered on his lips, disappearing before it could properly take root. "What do you normally do? Romantic dates? Friendship that becomes more?"

Sensing he wasn't particularly interested in the answer, I didn't bother to give one. "And this house... it's..." I shrugged, unable to put what I wanted to say into words.

He turned his back, pulling the curtain open a few inches to stare out onto the street. "It's just a house. No less. No more."

"Well, yes... but—"

He swung back around. "Anyway, we didn't come here to talk about the house. Or to talk at all." He smiled, this one a practiced, seductive smile designed to make men go weak at the knees. I couldn't speak for all men, but it definitely had the desired effect on me, my cock already stirring. Despite that, I found myself longing for a different sort of smile. Like the one he'd suppressed earlier for reasons known only to himself.

Gaze locked on mine, he slowly pulled his shirt over his head, standing still for my inspection. And inspect him I did, my gaze roving hungrily over the skin he'd exposed. I'd been right about the gymnast's build. He was lean, but not overly so, with smooth, tanned skin stretched over taut muscles.

His fingers traveled to the button on his jeans, undoing that and his zipper before stepping out of them. It left him clad in a pair of skimpy black briefs, the telltale white band of the Calvin Klein logo topping them. I stared unashamedly at the unmistakable bulge of his cock behind the scant material. He walked over to the bed, falling back on it, his legs dangling over the end, before leaning up on his elbows to stare hungrily at me. "Your turn. I want to see your body again."

Shaky legs moved me forward almost of their own accord, his words acting as a potent aphrodisiac. I halted at the edge of the bed. There was no question that I was going to do this. The sight stretched out in front of me was too seductive, too irresistible. He was all the fantasies I didn't know I'd had rolled up into one. And right now, he was looking at me like I was the answer to all his prayers. Never mind removing my shirt, I wanted to rip it off—anything to have those beautiful blue eyes roving over my body again. Forgoing the ripping, I undid the buttons in record time, shrugging it from my shoulders and letting it fall to the floor. I attacked my jeans at the same speed until I was left in tented boxers, my desire plain to see.

His gaze dropped and he slowly and deliberately licked his lips. "Take them off. I want to see you naked."

I obliged, the boxers joining the rest of my clothes on the floor.

"Turn around. I want to see if the back view is as impressive as the front."

Considering I'd had him down as not much of a talker, he was making up for it now. Normally, it was something that annoyed me during sex. But coming from him, there was something seductive about it. Probably something to do with the plummy accent, which if I'd been thinking with my brain instead of my dick, should have clued me in way before the house had to the fact that he was from a far more privileged background than I was. The house that I assumed he must have inherited. I normally avoided anyone with his sort of upbringing like the plague. As a manual laborer who worked hard for every single penny I earned, I didn't like to give anyone the chance to look down their nose at me and find me lacking.

I did as he'd asked, turning around to stand with my back to him, my naked ass on display. I smiled at his sharp intake of breath. Someone liked what they saw. Standing still, I let him look his fill, narrowly resisting the urge to flex. I could almost feel the heated gaze as it ran all over me. It felt like tiny pinpricks of sensation, heating my skin wherever it touched. Which was everywhere. He'd gone quiet, all his focus concentrated on his examination of the male form. My male form. I was suddenly glad of every bit of strenuous activity which had shaped those muscles he was so keen to admire. Figuring I'd given him long enough to stare, I turned back.

Tom sat up, his hands coming out to touch, skimming over my broad shoulders, down my biceps, and across my chest, his fingers leaving a trail of goosebumps across my skin. "You're gorgeous. All these muscles. It was one of the first things I noticed about you. You should see what they look like when you come. All tensed and twitching. It was beautiful."

"Is that why you approached me?"

Again, he suppressed a smile. I wanted to grab him and tease the corners of his mouth until they gave in to their instincts. He shook his head. "No. I approached you because you were looking at me as if you wanted to devour me. Pretty much the same way you're looking at me now." He lay down again, arms outstretched to the side like some sort of sacrificial lamb. "So have at it."

I didn't need any further invitation. Tumbling onto the bed next to him, I got my first touch of his bare skin as my fingers explored his chest, watching with fascination as the skin goose-bumped under my caress. If he was that responsive to a simple touch, what was it going to be like when I fucked him? I paused when my fingers reached the edge of the tight briefs he still wore. "Can I take these off?"

He nodded his assent, lifting his hips as I eased my fingers beneath the material. I pulled them down slowly, taking my time, the anticipation of seeing his cock making my own throb insistently. It was like unwrapping the best Christmas present ever. Then he was naked and I was staring down at an erect cock just as beautiful as the rest of him. I leaned over, keen to get my mouth on him and return the favor from earlier. The only issue I'd ever had was kneeling on the dirty floor.

To my surprise, he stopped me before I could get close. I frowned, lifting my gaze to his face. He shook his head, delivering one of those almost smiles again. "I won't last. I told you, you could fuck me." He hesitated, biting his lip. It was the first sign of nerves I'd seen from him. "Do you have... that is, I don't have..."

It took a moment to cotton on to what he was referring to. "Condoms?"

He nodded. "I... ran out."

I stroked my fingers over his bare arm, tracing the muscles there and finding it hard to stop touching him, my fingers almost magnetized to his skin. "I have one in my wallet." Reluctantly separating from him, I scrambled off the bed, locating my wallet in my discarded jeans and praying that there was indeed a condom in there. It had been a while since I'd gotten any action and I certainly hadn't anticipated tonight ending with the opportunity to fuck a gorgeous twink on a four-poster bed. My fingers closed around the familiar shape of a condom, and it was all I could do not to breathe a sigh of relief. There was also a packet of lube. Grabbing both and leaving my wallet lying on top of my jeans, I hastened back to the bed.

Tom had rolled over onto his front, his perfectly formed ass tipped up in a blatant invitation. He rolled his head to the side, bringing me into his line of sight. "I can't wait for you to bury that huge cock of yours in my ass."

That made two of us. I'd planned on more foreplay. Planned to spend time exploring his body and finding all the places which made him tremble. But all of that went out the window at his words. He wasn't just a talker. He was a dirty talker. Ripping the condom packet open, I carefully rolled it over my cock, adding extra lube from the packet. After all, there was no such thing as too much. Climbing back onto the bed, I straddled him, my sheathed cock resting between the two perfect globes of his ass. "Are you sure?"

He squirmed against me and I groaned. Taking the movement as a clear yes, I moved over him, pulling his ass cheeks apart and lining my cock up with the tight pucker it revealed. He gave another glance over his shoulder, his cheeks flushed with arousal. "Fuck me, Aiden. I want to feel you deep inside me. I want you to make me come."

I gave an experimental push, his body reacting the exact opposite to the words he'd just thrown at me. It was like trying to push into a vice. A vice that had clamped down so tight that nothing would fit into it, no matter how hard you tried. Gritting my teeth with the effort of holding back, I tried again with the exact same result. "Relax."

He gave a strangled gasp. "It's fine. Do it."

Even as aroused as I was, there was no way I was going to cause him pain. I reached for the packet of lube I'd left lying on the side of the bed. Using one well-lubed finger, I traced around his hole, the skin quivering under my touch. Satisfied he'd relaxed enough, I pushed gently. Even with just the one finger, Tom was uncomfortably tight. Exhibiting far more patience than my body wanted me to, I concentrated on working the digit slowly in and out, trying to get him to loosen up. Worried he'd gone quiet, I raised my head while I continued to thrust into him, only to find he'd buried his head in the pillow. "Tom?"

He lifted up slightly, just enough that I could hear him speak. "What?"

I smiled at the defensive note in his voice. "Are you ready for two fingers?"

"I was ready for you to fuck me."

"Your body wasn't."

"Fuck my body!"

A laugh escaped from my throat. "That's what we're trying to do." Taking it slowly, I attempted to introduce a second finger. But again, his body clamped down, tension reflecting in his muscles. I removed my finger and sat back. "Turn over."

"You haven't fucked me yet."

I patted him on the ass. "Not going to happen. You're way too wound up tonight." I tried to pick my words carefully so as not to offend. "Maybe you've got things on your mind. Work. Something else. I don't know. But, it's fine."

He flipped over so fast, it was all I could do to keep my balance on the bed as it rocked. "Don't leave."

I removed the condom, choosing to drop it on top of my jeans rather than onto the luxurious cream-colored carpet. Tom hadn't lost his erection so at least that was something. Emptying out the rest of the lube sachet into my palm, I came down on top of him, my larger body notching into his perfectly. Almost like we were made for each other. "I'm not going anywhere. There's other things we can do." I maneuvered our bodies to the perfect position where I could wrap a hand around both of our cocks at the same time.

He thrust his hips, pushing his cock into my grip, his body quickly getting on board with the idea, even if the words out of his mouth belied that. "I said you could fuck me."

Thrusting so that our cocks slid together in just the right way, I tried to concentrate on the conversation we were apparently going to have in the middle of getting off. "You didn't sign a contract. I'm not going to sue you." I broke off, as after a halting start, we managed to find the perfect rhythm. "Just like that! God, yeah, that feels good."

For the next few minutes, there was no more conversation. There was only the sound of our bodies moving together, combined with the ragged breathing and heavy moans of two men approaching orgasm.

As we both got closer, our movements became a lot less coordinated. I held back, wanting him to come first, the strain in my muscles from holding myself above him without putting too much of my weight on him almost too much. His chest flushed, his face twisting as his cock pulsed over both of our abdomens. Letting go of his softening cock and closing my eyes, I used his cum as extra lube, stroking myself quickly while replaying the images of how he'd looked when he came. I gasped as I shot over his stomach, my eyes jerking open to find him watching me.

He ran a finger through our combined loads bringing it to his mouth to taste. If I hadn't already come twice that night, that sight alone would have had me gearing up for another round. Muscles fatigued beyond belief, I rolled to the side, breathing hard.

His voice when it came was hesitant. "You were right."

I rolled my head toward him to find him staring up at the ceiling. "About what?"

"We didn't need to fuck."

I waited for further clarification, but none came.

He sat up suddenly. "I'm thirsty. Are you thirsty? We should get a drink. You want a drink, right?" Without waiting for an answer, he reached over the side of the bed, retrieving his shirt from the floor and using it to wipe himself off before throwing it my way. I glanced around the room, hoping for an alternative but there wasn't one. Come to think of it, the room was fairly bare. No towels. No nothing, really, apart from the furniture and the bedding. Shrugging, I went ahead and used his shirt. After all, it already had Tom's cum on it so adding a bit more wasn't going to make much of a difference. And it seemed a shower wasn't in the cards. Not yet anyway. As for Tom, he was already on his feet and fastening his jeans. I hurried to catch up with him, getting dressed almost as fast as I'd undressed.

Chapter Three

The kitchen was of course huge, with every gadget you could think to name and a few that I couldn't have named if I tried. Although, Tom's aversion to light might have had something to do with that. At least, I assumed that was the reason he'd bypassed the switch on his way past. The only light source in the kitchen came from the refrigerator door he'd just opened. I pulled my gaze away from the bent-over jean-clad ass I'd never gotten to fuck as he glanced over his shoulder. "What do you want? Orange juice? Apple juice?" He pulled out a glass bottle, squinting at its label. "We've got beer apparently. Think it's some sort of German brand. No idea what it tastes like. I can't promise that it won't taste like shit. Or I could make you a tea or a coffee if you prefer?"

Hang on. We? Who was the *we* in that equation? I was gearing up to ask when the room was suddenly flooded with light. Having come from a darkened room, through a dark entrance hall, and into an equally dark kitchen, it took a while for my eyes to adjust. Still squinting, I was finally able to make out the woman dressed in silk standing in the doorway, her hand still hovering over the switch. I believed the correct word for what she was wearing was a negligee. She'd obviously been in bed before coming downstairs. The question was, who the hell was she? Was Tom married? My guts churned at the thought that I'd just been rolling around naked with a married man. Had I just helped him to cheat? The thought made me feel sick.

She gave me a disparaging once-over, contempt dripping from every pore, before walking over to the sink and filling a glass with water. Then she directed her attention toward Tom. "Darling. Where have you found this one? Are you doing this to try and annoy me?" Not waiting for a response, her gaze swept back in my direction. "Do you know how old he is?"

My blood ran cold, a rush of realizations hitting me all at the same time. This woman was far too old to be Tom's wife. The blue eyes giving me a cool stare, though, were eerily familiar. This was Tom's mother. Ergo, it wasn't his house at all. It was his parents' house. And that hadn't been his room either. The thing that had been niggling away at me suddenly became clear. There'd been no personal possessions in the room. I'd been so blinded by lust that I'd failed to notice it was a guest room. Why hadn't he taken me to his room? Panic seized a hold of me. *His age! Oh my God, what was his age?* You didn't fuck him, my subconscious screamed at me. Right, like that would stand up in court. The woman—Tom's mum—stood and watched the myriad emotions play across my face. Finally, she answered her own question with a haughty raise of one eyebrow. "Seventeen. You look to be in your thirties. Are you in the habit of seducing seventeen-year-old boys? I think there's a name for that."

"Oh, for Christ's sake!" Tom strode across the kitchen, coming to a halt a few steps away from his mother. "Are you serious? I'm eighteen. I didn't for one minute think you'd remember my birthday... my *eighteenth* birthday when it actually happened. But I thought that at some point in the last three weeks it might have dawned on you that you missed it, you know, given that you supposedly did give birth to me." He turned to me. "I'm eighteen. Sorry you had to—"

I didn't want to hear any more. The news that he was eighteen should have come as a relief. It didn't. That was still far too young, and years younger than I'd assumed. I was an idiot and the evidence of that was standing right in front of me, thirteen years my junior. "I need to go." I left the kitchen, heading blindly in the direction where I remembered the front door to be, thankful that I had all my clothes back on so I could just leave. And thank God I'd chosen the right direction as well, the front door unlocking from the inside.

"Aiden."

Ignoring Tom calling my name, I hurried down the driveway, pressing the button which released the gate from the inside and heading out onto the street. It wasn't until I'd walked hurriedly for a few minutes in a random direction that I registered that I didn't have a fucking clue where I was or how I was going to get home. I stopped dead, worried that in my haste I was heading in the opposite direction to where I needed to go.

A glance at my watch revealed it to be one in the morning. I cycled through a possible list of people I could call. My sister, Anabelle, would ask the fewest questions, but there was no way I could call her at this time. She was a single parent of a six-month-old baby. It would mean her having to bundle the baby in the car as well. JT was my closest friend, but unlike my sister, there would be questions galore. Most of my other contacts were work colleagues. None of them would be up for driving out in the middle of the night to pick me up.

I pulled my phone out of my pocket, shaking my head at the red battery icon, indicating low battery. *Fucking great.* I could call a cab, but it was doubtful I had sufficient money on me to pay the fare. It seemed like my only option was to walk. Praying the battery would hold out for long enough for me to at least get my bearings, I opened up the maps app and set about trying to work out the best route to take. I winced as the search brought up the bad news that I was over nine miles from home. It was going to take me a couple of hours to walk that far, and that was assuming I didn't manage to get lost along the way.

A black cab drew up alongside me, the driver rolling the window down before leaning across.

Before he could speak, I got in there first. "Much as your services would be welcome, I've got no money, mate."

"Are you Aiden?"

I nodded, my confusion no doubt written across my face as I tried to work out how some random cabbie could possibly know my name. Did I know him? Did he used to work on the building site? We had a few guys come in, work there for a couple of weeks, before realizing that manual labor wasn't for them. It was possible his stint could have been so short-lived I'd forgotten him.

He scratched at his beard. "Weirdest dispatch call I've ever had. Can you search for some guy on the streets around here? All I was given was a vague physical description, including"—he gestured toward my jacket—"that you were wearing a black jacket. Nearly drove straight past you. It's a miracle I found you." He rifled through a pile of papers on the dashboard until he found a leaflet. "Hang on. There was a message." He turned the leaflet over to reveal a couple of sentences scribbled in blue biro on the back and proceeded to read them out. "Sorry about my mum. Least I can do is make sure you get home safely. It's signed by someone called Tom." He looked up. "Mean anything to you?"

I nodded again, unsure how I felt about Tom being considerate enough to worry about how I was getting home. The cabbie tapped his fingers impatiently on the dashboard. "Listen, mate. Are you getting in or not? I've already spent about fifteen minutes looking for you. I'm meant to be clocking off soon."

"I don't have any money... only change." I tapped my pockets as if to illustrate the fact.

"It's all paid for."

"Yeah?"

"Yeah." He checked his watch again.

I got in. An hour and a half walk or a twenty-five-minute cab journey that was already paid for. I was proud but I wasn't stupid.

Chapter Four

I put the last load of bricks down, massaging my sore left shoulder and feeling ancient. It probably had more to do with the fact that I'd gotten a grand total of five hours of sleep last night by the time the cab dropped me off in front of my house. The one-bedroom ground-floor flat seeming ridiculously tiny and shabby after the house in Richmond.

"Hey!"

I grimaced at the volume of JT's voice as it carried right across the building site. I watched him walk across the yard, two matching Tupperware containers clutched in his beefy hands. He shoved one at my chest. "Here. Juliana made curry. She wants you to eat it as well so that you can tell her how wonderful it is the next time you see her." Despite my fatigue, I smiled. Juliana often sent enough food for both of us. How JT had ever managed to convince the tiny, gorgeous lady to marry a great big, hulking brute like him, I had no idea. Even on their wedding day, I'd half expected her to do a runner. Instead she'd stared up at him as if he were her whole world and I'd experienced a distinct pang of jealousy as they'd exchanged their handwritten wedding vows, wondering when I was going to get to meet someone special who'd look at me with even an ounce of the feelings they had for each other. Two years later and they were still going strong and talking about trying for a baby. And I was no closer to finding my soulmate.

JT gestured over to the nearby wall, indicating we should take a seat. "Already heated it up. You just need to eat."

Knowing argument was futile, I planted my ass on the wall, pulling the lid from the Tupperware and taking a big sniff. "Wow! Smells amazing."

JT held out a fork and I took it eagerly, digging straight in. He sighed. "I swear she cooks for you, rather than me."

Mouth full, I settled for rolling my eyes. There was no way that was true. She adored him. We ate in companionable silence, both of us shaking our heads at the attempt happening in front of us to attach antlers to one of the diggers. Our containers were both empty by the time they'd conceded defeat, settling for winding silver tinsel around the cab instead. Lord knows why they felt the need to decorate the building site every year. I put the lid back on and passed it back to JT, knowing that Juliana would want it back.

JT took it, placing both containers next to him on the wall. "So, now you've eaten. How about telling me what's got you acting like a bear with a sore head today?"

I shrugged. "Don't know what you mean? I'm fine."

His face said it all. "So, you didn't call our sixteen-year-old work-experience boy an idiot because he didn't pick up brick-laying in twenty seconds flat?"

"I apologized." I sounded defensive even to my own ears. It hadn't been like me. Normally, I was the model of patience. It was one of the reasons that the newbies were often asked to shadow me. But, something about the boy this morning had grated.

"Has this got anything to do with you disappearing last night?"

I frowned. "Disappearing? I was at the pub."

JT crossed his arms. "You *were* at the pub. Then you weren't there when I got there. Then you didn't respond to my message. Then—" He held a finger up when it looked like I was going to interrupt him. "—you weren't at home either because I tried there in case you were thinking of lying. Oh, and you weren't at your sister's either because I called and asked. I assumed you'd pulled. But, given your mood today, I'm not so sure now."

I contemplated how much to tell him. We'd been friends for ten years and he was the least judgmental person I knew. If I didn't speak to him, who else was I going to talk to? "I did something stupid. Really stupid."

His face creased into a pronounced frown. "Like what? It's nothing criminal, is it?"

I shook my head. "No. But now I'm wondering why you'd think that."

He laughed. "You've always looked dodgy. Thought you might have come up with a way of making extra money that wasn't entirely above board."

"You were closer originally."

He thought for a moment, sudden comprehension dawning. "You pulled! But, hang on, I don't get the link between that and doing something stupid. You deserve to get laid once in a while, man. You're not a monk."

"He turned out to be... posh... and rich... and..."

"And what?"

I sighed. "Young."

"How young?"

I cast my eye around the building site, using it as an excuse to avoid JT's gaze. It was pretty empty, the rest of the workers having the good sense to get out of the early December cold and eat their lunch in the mobile cabin. "Eighteen." I risked a glance across to my friend, relieved when he didn't recoil in shock at my announcement.

"I'll admit it's a bit of an age gap. Are you going to see him again?"

My laugh of utter disbelief escaped in a rush. "No, I'm not going to see him again. What do you think I am? If I'd known he lived in a huge house in Richmond and was only eighteen, I wouldn't have gone anywhere near him."

JT stood, moving in front of me so I was forced to look up at him. "Which bit bothers you the most? The fact that he's rich or the fact that he's eighteen?"

"What? Both? Neither? I don't know. Stop trying to confuse me."

He grinned. "Seems to me like you should stop beating yourself up over it. It happened. You can't turn the clocks back, so"—he shrugged—"just forget about it." He turned to go before pausing. "Oh, couple of things. Maybe stay away from the work-experience guy this afternoon, his... extreme youth seems to be giving you flashbacks."

I rolled my eyes. "And the second thing?"

"We're going to the pub tonight. You owe me a beer for all the chasing around I did last night searching for you."

. . ⚬⚬ . .

JT THREW A PEANUT IN the air, leaned his head back, and caught it in his mouth. I glared at him. "Do you have to do that?"

He nodded. "Not allowed to do it at home. Jules complained when she found some on the floor."

"I wonder why. I bet she..." I suddenly froze with my pint of beer halfway to my mouth. Instead of drinking it, I banged it straight back down on the table, some of it sloshing over the side. "You have got to be fucking kidding me." It had been hard enough getting the previous night out of my head, especially when I was back in the same pub. The visit to the bathroom in particular had brought a rush of unwanted memories. But now I was either seeing things or the other participant in those memories had just walked through the door. He scanned the lounge, his gaze alighting on me.

JT turned to see what I was staring at, a huge smirk appearing when he faced me again. "Is that him?"

I gave a nod, my throat suddenly dry. "Shit! He's coming over."

JT let out a huge bellow of laughter. "Course he is. He's obviously searching for you." He leaned over the table, lowering his voice. "By the way, if it helps, he does not look eighteen. Definitely looks older. He does, however, look rich. Have you seen the Rolex he's wearing? Didn't you notice that last night?"

Tom was already halfway across the room. "I wasn't exactly focusing at his wrist." *At least not that one.* I distinctly remembered staring at the other one as his hand was wrapped around my cock while he sucked it, though.

JT winked. "I bet you weren't. You dirty dog." He was stopped from saying anything else by Tom's arrival at the table.

I took a large gulp of beer, attempting to look anywhere but at the man in front of me.

Tom was silent for a moment before finally speaking. "Aiden, can I talk to you?"

JT had already risen to his feet before I got a chance to respond. "Well, this sounds like my cue to go and lose on the quiz machine. I'll be over there if you need me." He winked before sauntering off.

And then it was just the two of us, Tom continuing to hover nervously by the side of the table. Sighing, I waved him into the chair JT had just vacated. He sank into it gratefully, as if I was doing him a huge favor, and I looked at him properly for the first time since he'd entered the pub. God! He was pretty. It was no wonder I'd been so blinded by lust the previous night that I hadn't been able to think clearly. That was my excuse anyway, and I was sticking to it. "I don't see what we've got to talk about."

Tom plucked the beer mat from the table and began to fiddle with it, turning it over and over in his hand, the light glinting off his watch with the movement. "Well, firstly, I wanted to say sorry. You know, about my mum. She was mean. I'm used to it, but she shouldn't have been rude to you. There was no call for it."

"You don't think she's got a right to be annoyed about you parading men in front of her nose in the middle of the night?"

He dropped the beer mat, his head rearing up to look me dead in the eye. "Men?"

I wilted under the intense stare, the blue eyes a lot more formidable when they weren't tinged with arousal. "I can't remember her exact words, but that was definitely her insinuation. She said something about you trying to annoy her."

"So... you think I take a long line of men back to my house, night after night?"

I shrugged, glancing over to where JT stood by the quiz machine. He wasn't even pretending to use it. Just leaning against it while he blatantly watched us. I averted my gaze as he gave me a double-thumbs-up. "I don't know. I don't know you. Do you?"

"No! Christ, you of all people should know that's crap."

I frowned, running my hand through my hair wearily and wondering why the hell I hadn't stayed home tonight. Actually, the previous night would have helped as well. "Why would I know that? I don't understand."

He stared at me for the longest time, his mouth tightening. "Because you must have been able to tell that I was... I am..." He lowered his voice, checking that no one was in hearing distance before speaking again. "You know."

I shook my head.

"A virgin."

It was like being punched in the chest by a wrecking ball. A lot of things from the previous night suddenly making a hell of a lot more sense. He'd been tight. Too tight. I'd put it down to stress, or it having been a long time. Not once had it ever occurred to me that he'd never done it before. Why would it? Virgins didn't pick people up and blow them in bathrooms. They didn't talk dirty like he did either. But despite the evidence to the contrary, I believed him. There was no faking the way he'd reacted, and there was no faking the look of flushed embarrassment he wore now. "But you were going to... you kept telling me to..." I took another large gulp of beer. "Fuck!"

"I wanted you to be my first."

I stared at him in amazement. "You don't even know me."

His gaze continued to bore into mine. "I liked you. I *like* you."

"We barely even talked. *You* didn't want to talk."

He did the almost smile thing again. "Sometimes you don't need to talk. You just know. It felt right."

This conversation was getting crazier by the minute. I had no idea how I was supposed to respond so I stayed silent.

Tom sighed. "Can I ask you a question?"

"Only if I get to ask you one as well."

He looked uncomfortable before nodding his agreement. "I know you like me too. You told me last night that you don't normally do that sort of thing. So why did you leave so suddenly last night? Be honest. Is it the fact that my parents are rich? Or my age?"

It was pretty much the same question JT had asked me that afternoon. "How old do you think I am?"

I tried not to squirm as Tom slowly scanned all of the parts of me he could see that weren't hidden by the table. "Late twenties?"

"Your mum was right. I'm in my thirties. Thirty-one."

"So?" He accompanied the question with a delicate raise of one eyebrow.

"You don't think that's way too old?"

He combined a shake of his head with an eye roll. "Age is just a number." He leaned forward, the seductive expression from last night back in full force. "Want to go to the bathroom again?"

"Why don't you ever smile?"

He sat back, all traces of seduction dropping away. "What do you mean? I smile."

I felt like I'd touched a nerve. I had two options. Let it drop or try and get an honest answer out of him. I went for the latter. "Not really. Not genuine smiles. Sometimes, you look like you're going to and then it's like you stop yourself."

His lashes came down, hiding his gaze for a few seconds. "Maybe I don't have an awful lot to smile about."

A snort of disbelief escaped from my mouth before I could stop it. "Yeah, it must be dreadful having all that money."

"Money isn't everything."

"And that sentence only ever gets said by people who have a lot of it."

He tilted his head to the side. "I tell you what. I have a boat. Come and spend some time on it this weekend. Just as friends. Maybe you can make me smile."

Was he for real? "It's December. It's freezing. Or is boat a codeword for fully heated yacht?"

"No, it's definitely a boat." He paused, challenge sparking in his steady gaze. "I never had you down as such a wuss. Big, strong man like you. What is it you're scared of, the water or the cold? Or that you won't be able to keep your hands off me?"

I bristled at the insult, which was precisely the reaction he'd been after. He held out a pen, together with the beer mat he'd been fiddling with. I regarded the items with a great deal of suspicion. "What's that for?"

"Your number. Write it down so we can arrange times for the weekend."

When I didn't immediately take the items from him, he laid them down in front of me and waited. I stared at the pen, my brain firing off a number of reasons I should refuse. *He was eighteen. He still lived with his parents. He was loaded, his watch probably cost more than I made in a month. Our lives were a million worlds apart. Add a few more years and I'd be old enough to be his father.*

One other sentence kept repeating over and over again, the words he'd just said to me. *Maybe you can make me smile.* I cast a surreptitious glance across the table at him, noting that the nerves from earlier seemed to be back. *Was he that scared of being rejected?*

Even looking so serious, he was gorgeous. I dreaded to think how devastatingly attractive he could be if he really did smile. I wanted to find out though. And like he said, it was just as friends. I had willpower. Contrary to what Tom seemed to think, I was more than capable of keeping my hands and everything else off him. Last night had been an aberration where I hadn't had all the necessary information. And I'd nipped it in the bud as soon as I'd discovered his age. I picked up the pen and wrote my number on the beer mat.

Chapter Five

I stared down at the small wooden boat, its oars resting on the side. "This is your boat?"

Tom climbed in, his step from the jetty sure-footed like he'd done it a thousand times. He balanced with his hands held out to the side. "This is my boat. Told you it wasn't a yacht."

"It's tiny."

"It's big enough for two." He eased himself onto the seat and grasped the oars, his breath misting in the freezing cold air.

"If I fall in, I'll get hypothermia and die."

"Don't fall in, then."

I glanced back down the towpath, its sole occupant a lone man walking his dog. It was difficult to remember why I'd ever agreed to this. My very short history with Tom seemed to be an ever-growing list of things I shouldn't do.

"Do you need help getting in? Is that the problem? I could hold your hand."

I leveled a glare Tom's way. Despite the fact that I knew he was taking great delight in winding me up deliberately, I couldn't help but rise to it. "No, I don't need help getting in. I'm just deciding if this is really how I intend to spend my afternoon."

Tom stiffened, turning his face away to stare out over the river. "I didn't *make* you come here. If you want to go, go. I'm not stopping you."

Great! Now, I'd managed to offend him. I stepped into the boat gingerly, careful not to overbalance. "I'm here now." The boat was so small that it only took another step to reach the seat facing Tom. I lowered myself onto it, huddling into my jacket and wishing I'd brought a better coat. Or a pair of gloves. Or a hat, seeing as my head was freezing. Tom, of course, had all three, his beanie hat pulled down low over his ears.

Using the oars, he pushed the boat out toward the center of the river. The silence stretched between us until I couldn't take it any longer. I didn't if

Tom was still annoyed at my reluctance to take part in an activity I'd previously agreed to, or if he was just one of those people who alternated between talking a lot and then saying nothing. But it was like the back of the cab all over again. "Is this what you do with your friends?"

He lifted his gaze to mine momentarily, his mouth twisting into a tight line. "What friends?"

I laughed. "Oh, come on, you must have friends. Everyone has friends."

He sat back, allowing the boat to drift. "I guess it depends on what your definition of friends is?"

I tucked my chin into my jacket, my hands pushed as far as they could go into the pockets in an effort to keep them warm. "I don't know. People who you can trust. That you like spending time with. That you can rely on. People who like doing the same things as you. You know, common interests?"

"That man you were with the other day in the pub. Is he a friend?"

"JT. Yeah. We've been friends for years. We work together on the building site. I'm friends with both him and his wife."

"I don't have anyone like that."

The statement was delivered in such a matter-of-fact way that I floundered for a moment for something to say. "Why not?"

He shrugged, his shoulders hunching almost all the way to his ears.

"What about people you went to school with?" I laughed drily. "It's not as if it was that long ago."

He turned to gaze out over the river, his breath fogging as he exhaled. "There was a group of us that hung out together."

"Well, there you go—friends."

"Until I decided that I didn't want to spend every single night sniffing so many lines of coke that I couldn't even remember my own name. Why do you think I'm so good at getting down on my knees in a bathroom stall? Coke makes you horny."

The words from anyone else would have been disturbing. From an eighteen-year-old, they were doubly so. I did my best to keep my face blank. Whatever his reasons for telling me this, sitting in judgment wasn't going to help. Besides, it would be hypocritical seeing as I'd been quite happy to be the recipient of one of those blow jobs.

I sought desperately for some sort of positive spin I could put on what he'd said. "You've been talking past tense. Does that mean you've stopped? That you don't do coke anymore?"

He tugged at the finger of one of his gloves. "Yeah, I stopped. The night that I sniffed so much coke that I woke up in the gutter. And not one of those so-called friends had stuck around to check if I was okay. Or even bothered to call me the next day. I guess you could say it gave me the wake-up call I needed. They were annoyed at me for a while. But, do you want to know why?"

"Why?" I had an awful feeling I already knew what he was going to say.

His mouth twisted like some sort of awful imitation of a smile. "I paid for most of the coke."

I didn't bother to try and hide my wince. "What about your parents? They must have wondered where you were?"

His bitter laugh rang out across the empty water. "You'd think, wouldn't you?" He looked like he was going to say more but then stopped himself with a tiny shake of his head.

"Tom. I—"

He held his hand up. "Don't. I don't need your pity. That's not why I'm telling you any of this. I don't really know why I am. You asked about friends. I guess I'm explaining why none of those people were actual friends." He sat up, straightening his shoulders. "Anyway, I didn't bring you out here to depress you."

"Why did you bring me here?"

He dropped his gaze to stare down at the bottom of the boat, contemplating the question for far longer than it deserved, as if there were more than one answer and he was deciding which one to give. "You're meant to be making me smile, remember?"

"Well, I'm doing an absolute piss-poor job of it so far, aren't I?" I shivered, unable to stop the involuntary movement.

"You were right."

I raised a questioning eyebrow.

"It's too cold to be out here. Let's head back. Go for a drink or something instead." He grabbed the oars, steering the boat back in the direction of the river bank. As we got close, Tom lifted an arm to gesture at the corner post of the jetty. "Can you grab that? It's a pain to try and get the boat completely along-side."

"Anything to get out of this boat quicker to get somewhere warm."

My first mistake was standing up too fast, the boat rocking precariously be-neath my feet. The second was not recognizing quite how frozen my fingers were so that as I reached for the post, my grip was so poor that they simply slid straight off. I over-balanced, tipping over the side of the boat and stepping in-to the shallow water. The shock of the freezing cold water lapping around my thighs resulted in my third mistake. I stumbled backward, falling on my ass in the water and turning wet legs into a fully submerged body up to mid-chest. I gasped, my already cold body not appreciating the dunking one little bit.

I blamed the shock of everything happening so quickly for it taking me so long to register the sound of laughter. I looked up. Tom was standing in the boat, openly laughing at the dejected picture I must have made. When he saw my face, he made a supreme effort to stop. "I'm sorry. I'm sorry. It's not funny. Really, it's not. It's just..." His face creased up again, a bubble of laughter escap-ing. "You joked about falling in, and then..." He coughed before forcing himself to take a deep, calming breath.

I sat in the frozen water, staring up at him, only one thought foremost in my mind. "I made you smile."

His face stilled. "Yeah, you did. Only next time, perhaps think about using less drastic measures." He stepped nimbly from the boat—which of course had drifted perfectly alongside the jetty without any intervention—and quickly se-cured it before holding out his hand. "Come on, you idiot. Don't just sit there. Out of the freezing cold water."

I eyed Tom's hand, considering pulling him in and seeing how much he liked it. He probably wouldn't find it so funny then. He was eighteen, though. I didn't need to be pulling eighteen-year-olds into rivers no matter how amusing they might find my mishap. I took his hand and let him pull me out, my teeth chattering uncontrollably as I stood and dripped onto the wooden panels of the jetty. "Now what?"

"We go back to mine and get you dry before you actually do get hypother-mia." He paused at the dubious expression on my face. "My dad's away on busi-ness and I expect my mum's out shopping, or drinking, or getting her hair done. She's hardly ever there. It's only a ten-minute walk. You can't go home like that on the tube." He grabbed my arm, dragging me in the direction we needed to go. "Put these on." He passed over his hat, gloves, and scarf, ignoring all my protests until I gave in and wore them.

.. ⤞ ..

IT SEEMED STRANGE TO willingly return to a house that I'd recently fled from. I hoped Tom was right about his mother not being there since I didn't fancy another run-in with her. Once was more than enough. At least the house was lovely and warm when we entered. I guessed they didn't have to worry about not being able to pay their heating bills. As Tom led me straight up the stairs, I couldn't help but replay unwanted images of the last time we'd taken a similar route together. "Are you going to take me to *your* room this time?"

His step faltered and he shot me a look of surprise. "What do you mean?"

"The other room wasn't yours. It didn't have any personal things in it. Even the most minimalist person has more stuff than that."

Tom grimaced, his face reflecting his indecision. He gave a half-smile before changing direction, revealing he had indeed been about to try and pull the same trick twice. "Busted. Promise you won't laugh."

"At what?"

He didn't answer, continuing to move farther along the hallway until he reached a door on the left which he pushed open. I stepped inside to find myself confronted by a room that looked more like an art gallery than a bedroom, almost every inch of it, with the exception of the bed, covered in different-sized framed canvases—most of which were leaned against the wall.

I blinked. "Wow! I guess you really like art?"

He shrugged, a casual movement of just the one shoulder. There was a stillness about him, almost like he was waiting for something. I was clueless as to what, though. When I didn't make any further comment, he seemed to snap out of it. I felt like I was missing something. Had he expected to be mocked for owning so many pictures? Most people collected something, whether it be keyrings or in Tom's case something much bigger. He walked to the other side of the room, flinging a connecting door open. "Bathroom's through here. While you shower, I'll put your clothes in the washer."

Desperate to get out of the damp clothes as soon as I could, I headed straight there. Rather than moving out of the way, Tom remained in the doorway. It meant I either had to brush past him or wait for him to move. Not wanting to initiate the body contact needed for the former, I settled for waiting.

Tom turned slightly, his gaze sweeping over me from head to toe. "Can I watch?"

I shook my head, tamping down on the immediate wave of desire that flickered to life at the thought of soaping myself with an audience. And not just any audience, but one who I'd already been intimate with. He'd watch and then he'd probably join me in the shower and we could... *Eighteen. He's eighteen.* I needed to keep reminding myself of that fact. "Tom, I..."

He stepped aside, both hands held up in mock surrender. "Hey, you can't blame a guy for trying. And I did only say watch. That was really restrained of me considering I'd much rather touch. Surely, I get brownie points for that?"

Deciding it was better to say nothing, I took the opportunity to step inside and close the door behind me. No lock. Of course there wasn't; it was an ensuite. The voice when it came, sounded awfully close to the door, almost like Tom had pressed himself against it. "Pass your clothes through once you've taken them off. I promise not to look. Much."

I began the difficult task of struggling out of wet jeans, doing my best to ignore the running commentary outside the bathroom.

"...you're forgetting that I've already seen your body. And touched it. And sucked your cock. So there's really no need to be shy. Maybe that should be the rental fee for use of the shower, getting to see your cock again. You could jack off and I could watch and maybe offer some suggestions to improve the experience. Like..."

"Tom!" My voice was laden with a clear warning, my unruly cock already reacting to his words. If he added any more details, I wasn't sure I'd have the willpower to avoid dragging him in here. Tom always seemed happy not to say much unless he was talking dirty and then it seemed like the floodgates suddenly opened. Naked, apart from my briefs, I let my head rest against the door, struggling for control.

There was a long period of silence before he spoke. "Fine. I'll keep my fantasies to myself from now on if it makes you happy. If you'd hurried up and given me your clothes though, I wouldn't be out here with nothing else to think about except for you being naked. I'd be downstairs doing laundry. So it's your fault really."

He had a point. I quickly stepped out of my briefs, adding them to the pile and making sure that when I opened the door to hand them to Tom, I was firmly positioned behind it.

Tom took them from me with a smirk and I heard his footsteps cross the room as I closed the door again. I contemplated the shower. Hot water would definitely be welcome but if even his words aroused me this much, I wasn't sure how I'd fare if I ended up confronted by a naked Tom determined to squeeze in there with me. In the end, I settled on taking a quick one.

Luckily, the controls were straightforward to figure out. I showered in record time, despite the fact that it had to be one of the best showers I'd ever taken. I'd probably have given my left kidney for access to power jets like those after a day spent on the building site. To my relief, the door stayed closed. And if there was a slight feeling of something akin to disappointment stirring in my guts, then I did my best to ignore it.

Stepping out of the shower stall, I groaned aloud at the sight of the tiny white towel. I desperately searched for an alternative. But that was it. It was that or nothing. It barely covered my ass when I wrapped it around me. If it hadn't been impossible for Tom to have engineered me falling into the river, I might have suspected some kind of set-up.

Reminding myself he'd seen it all before anyway, I steeled myself and opened the door into the bedroom. Tom was seated on the bed. He turned his head as I approached, his blue eyes growing wide. "Wow! Those towels always seem a lot bigger on me."

Doing my best to appear nonchalant, I headed for a chair across the other side of the room. There was no way in hell I was going to sit next to him on the bed. That would be asking for trouble. "How long will my clothes take?"

Tom raised an eyebrow in a knowing fashion. "An hour or two." He didn't bother to hide it as he perused my bare chest. "So we need to think of something we can do for a couple of hours. Something that doesn't need clothes. Any suggestions?"

"Not that." My voice sounded surprisingly firm, given the turmoil going on inside my head. It would be so easy to give in. Agreeing to meet him today had been a huge mistake in retrospect. There was no way in hell I was going to compound it by making an even bigger one. I didn't even blame him for being pushy. He was eighteen. If he was anything like I'd been at that age, he was a walking ball of hormones who only thought about one thing. Circumstances had delivered me half-naked in his bedroom so of course he was going to try and capitalize on it.

It came as a surprise then when he simply dropped his gaze to the floor, studying it as if the meaning of life was hidden somewhere in the fibers of the carpet. When he raised his head and his blue eyes met mine, there was resignation written there. "I get it, Aiden. You're not interested. You're hung up on my age. Unfortunately, I can't make myself older... so..." He shrugged, his gaze returning to the floor. "Seeing as sex is off the table, how about a cup of tea?"

Stunned into silence by his easy capitulation, it took a few seconds before I could force a nod of agreement. Tea sounded a lot safer. Tom stood, the almost smile making a return. It pained me to see it again. He paused by the door. "Wait here. I don't think my parents will be back, but I know you don't want to be bumping into them dressed like that. So it's probably safer... just in case."

I nodded again, turning my attention to the paintings in the bedroom once he'd left. They were mostly landscapes, the bold brushstrokes depicting everything from a beach to a country cottage. Whoever had painted them clearly had an awful lot of talent, yet each picture held a slightly gloomy quality. I couldn't work out why. Even the ones painted in bright colors seemed to be missing something. Perhaps it was the absence of people. Or maybe it was just a collective effect of the pictures being placed so haphazardly around the room. A stack of unframed canvases had been turned to face the wall, hiding whatever was painted on them. My curiosity piqued, I was leaning over to turn one around when Tom walked back into the room, two steaming mugs held in his hands. "Don't touch those!"

I snatched my hand back as if I'd been caught doing something I shouldn't. Which I guess I had really. He might have given me access to his bedroom but he hadn't given me carte blanche to go snooping. "Sorry. I just wondered why they were facing the other way."

He passed one of the mugs over. "I didn't know how you took it. I went for milk, no sugar."

I took the mug from him, being careful to make sure our fingers didn't touch. "That's fine."

His gaze flicked back to the paintings. "The artist doesn't want anyone to see those ones."

I nodded as if that made perfect sense. It didn't. I couldn't see why someone would be happy for someone to see some of their paintings and not the rest. "Who's the artist?"

His gaze swung to mine, amusement lurking in the depths of his gaze. "Some fucking headcase. You wouldn't like him if you met him."

Frowning at the odd statement, I let the subject drop. Checking my watch revealed very little had gone past. There was still ages until my clothes would be ready. I had a feeling it might prove the longest couple of hours of my life.

Chapter Six

I paced restlessly in front of Hyde Park tube station, unable to fathom why I was there. When I'd left Tom's house the previous weekend, it was with a strange note of sadness that I wouldn't see him again, with my feelings reflected in his expression.

So it was hard to work out how I'd managed to get from that point to meeting him again a week later—all in the space of a few text messages. It could only be guilt, right?

At least this time I was dressed appropriately for the weather and we were nowhere near a river. With Christmas just a week away, I was still cold though, even with a big coat, scarf, and gloves on. I'd foregone a hat. I'd never been much of a fan. And after Tom had used all his powers of persuasion to get me there, he was late. We'd said six. It was nearly ten past. Was I about to get stood up by a teenager?

And then there he was in front of me, his cheeks flushed with the cold and looking just as handsome as I remembered. He cocked his head to one side, regarding me earnestly. "What's got you looking so grumpy?"

"You're late."

"*Slightly* late. What else?"

I let out a sigh, deciding to go with brutal honesty. "I have no idea why I agreed to do this."

"Because it's me? Or because it's Winter Wonderland?"

I rolled my eyes. Even the name was cheesy as hell. "Isn't it for kids?"

He crossed his arms and waited silently.

I frowned, unsure what the dramatic pause was supposed to be about. "What?"

"I was waiting for some crack about me being one. You know, because of my age. That you're so hung up on."

"I don't see you as a kid. We..." I lowered my voice in case any passersby exiting the tube were listening. "...did stuff. Well, you know... you were there."

His lips curled into a smile. A genuine one. I wanted to punch the air in victory. I hadn't even had to fall into a river for that one, just agree that he wasn't a kid.

The smile grew wider still. "I most certainly was. I remember it well." He stepped into my space but I refused to give him the satisfaction of taking a step back and putting distance between us. "I expect I'll remember it many times for years to come. I expect I'll remember it every time I'm alone in bed at night, and need to—"

I gave in, backing away and putting some much-needed space between us before he could go into the type of graphic detail that would have my cock sitting up and taking far more notice than it should. "I get the drift. If we're doing this, let's go."

He fell into step beside me as we followed the throng of people already heading toward Hyde Park. I could hear the music and see the lights even from a distance. "Why here?"

Tom shrugged his shoulders. "Why not? It'll be fun."

"For who?"

He rounded on me, his eyes glinting with amusement. "Both of us, if you relax a bit. You're thirty-one, not eighty-one. Besides, I've wanted to come here for years."

"Your friends didn't..." I stopped, remembering what he'd told me when we were in the boat. *Nice one, Aiden. Put your foot in it, why don't you?* "Not their scene I guess?"

He pulled a face. "Yeah! Distinct lack of class A drugs."

"What about your parents? It's been going for years. They didn't bring you when you were younger?"

Tom sighed. "My parents? No. It wouldn't even have crossed their minds."

We stepped through the huge archway that served as an entrance. There was no entrance fee. It was a good thing really. I'd probably have used it as an excuse to leave. I spent a moment taking stock of my surroundings. It was all lights, noise, and people, the sound of the crowd mixing with the music and the screams from the fairground rides. There was a multitude of smells as well from sweet sugar to the more acidic smell of fried onions. The whole thing was an assault on the senses, far removed from my usual evenings at The Royal Oak. "What are we supposed to do here?"

Tom spun round in a small circle, his arms outstretched and his blue eyes gleaming. "Everything. Rides. Food. Drinks. Games. We're going to do it all. You're not really going to be a grump, are you?"

He seemed happier than I'd ever seen him before. Who was I to spoil that? I could either continue treating this whole thing with an air of cynicism or I could make an effort to loosen up. I thrust my hands deeper into my pockets. "I'm not a grump. It's just that it's the middle of December, the temperature's close to zero, and you keep dragging me outside to do stuff."

Tom stepped closer, his voice dropping to a husky whisper. "Just say the word and I'll be only too happy to warm you up."

He was already heating up certain parts of my anatomy. That was part of the problem. It didn't take much more than a suggestive glance from him for my cock to remind me how much fun I'd had with Tom before I'd discovered certain things about him. I should probably be relieved that we were in the midst of a crowd. It stopped him from dragging me away somewhere where he could work his magic with seductive looks and honeyed words. Back in his bedroom in Richmond, I'd thought he'd given up. But it seemed he'd just been regrouping before he planned his next attack.

I chose to ignore the sexual innuendo. He already knew how I felt about the age gap. There was no need to keep reiterating it. In fact, I was beginning to suspect that a lot of the flirting was because he reveled in seeing how uncomfortable and lost for words it left me. "Where to first?"

Despite my resolve, the disappointment on his face crushed me. I didn't like making anyone feel like that. I dimly remembered being eighteen and wanting to fuck anything that moved. That's all it was. I'd made the mistake of cruising him in the pub and making my interest all too clear, and now he'd imprinted on me like some sort of baby rabbit. A very sexy baby rabbit, but a baby rabbit nonetheless.

Once he realized that what had happened the other night couldn't, and wouldn't, happen again, then he'd turn his attention elsewhere. Hopefully to someone closer in age or at least on the right side of thirty. It didn't stop my gaze from dropping to his jean-clad ass though as he walked off in the direction of one of the rides and remembering what it had looked like naked. Naked and tipped up in invitation while he'd begged me to fuck him even though he was a virgin.

Tom was dangerous in a way I'd never encountered before. Which again begged the question, why was I there? Why put temptation directly in my path? It would be better to tell him that this was a bad idea and leave. Or cite some sort of emergency. Hell, I didn't have to tell him anything. It wasn't like I owed him.

He turned, his brow furrowing as he spotted that I hadn't moved from where he'd left me. "Are you coming?"

I was being ridiculous. A couple of hours in his company, letting him have some fun with a friend who wasn't after him for his money, wasn't going to hurt anybody. Then we could go our separate ways and one day we'd look back at our history as something amusing. Decision made, I dug my chin into my scarf, bracing myself against the bitter cold, and shuffled after him, finding him staring up at a ride. It consisted of a two-seated car like the kind you might find on a big wheel. Except rather than going around and around at a sedate speed, it launched you into the air like you were on a huge piece of elastic.

Tom grabbed my arm as the couple who'd just been strapped in braced themselves, an expression midway between anticipation and fear etched on both of their faces. "Watch."

I didn't particularly want to as I had an awful feeling what the watching was leading up to, and it wasn't laughing and agreeing what idiots they were. They both screamed as the mechanism kicked in and they flew toward the sky at a million miles an hour, only to come rushing back to the ground at an equal pace. I felt sick just watching them.

Tom smiled, his eyes shining with glee. "The queue's really short."

I was beginning to regret wanting to see that smile, given the type of things that seemed to bring it out, namely freezing cold river dunkings and death-defying rides. "Oh, I wonder why. Perhaps people have decided that they'd like to live a bit longer."

He stared at me speculatively. "Are you scared?"

"Scared!" I made a sound of complete and utter derision and then lied through my teeth. "Course not. Don't be ridiculous."

"So you'll come on the ride with me, then?"

I scanned the other rides in the vicinity, none of which seemed anywhere near as bad as this one. "Just thinking that maybe it's not the best one to start with." My gaze traveled to a nice, gentle-looking carousel, wishing there was some way of hypnotizing Tom into wanting to go on that instead.

"No, that's part of the plan. You go on the scariest ride first and then all the others don't seem so bad."

I dragged my eyes away from the carousel. "*All* the others? And whose plan is that exactly?"

He shrugged. "Well, *my* plan obviously. And of course we've got to go on everything. Just like you have to do rides before you do food and drink."

That part made sense. Less vomiting, I surmised. I winced as another ear-piercing scream rang out as another couple were launched into the air. "I don't know. I'm not really a rides sort of person. I'm more of a..." *Sitting in the pub and drinking a pint* type person. I waved a hand around. "...you know, more into culture and stuff."

His face fell. "I understand."

I'd disappointed him again. "You can still go on it. I'll watch."

He shook his head, his shoulders hunched. "It doesn't matter."

If he'd tried to persuade me or coerce me in any way, I would have been able to hold firm, but being the cause of such dejection when I had the power to stop it was more than I could take. I grabbed him as he started to turn away. "Wait." I glanced back at the elastic band of doom as Tom paused. *I could always close my eyes, right? How bad could it be?*

One of the ride's current occupants, a blonde woman, spilled off it on wobbly legs and promptly burst into tears. Okay, that answered that question. Pretty damn bad, apparently. I grabbed Tom's hand before I could think better of it and pulled him over to the booth where tokens were available to be purchased. "Let's do this. You're paying though. I'm not paying for my own death. And if I cry afterward like that woman did, you have to pretend not to notice."

Tom grinned. "I'll go one better and I'll wipe your tears away." He caught himself as if suddenly remembering that he was supposed to be flirting. "Or lick them away. Your choice."

It was far too short a time before we found ourselves strapped into the seat, the man who'd done the strapping backing away so that he was clear of the ride. I wondered if it was too late to ask for his credentials, or at least reassurance that he'd never lost anyone yet. The ride gave a lurch and I closed my eyes, praying for two things: one, that I'd survive and two, that I wouldn't make too much of a fool of myself. Tom's hand fastened over mine on the bar we both held. "Relax, it'll be—"

He didn't get to finish his thought as we were both catapulted into the air. I grabbed his hand, holding on to it for dear life as my stomach ended up somewhere over my head before being brought back to Earth with a bump. And then the whole thing repeated itself over and over until I was no longer sure which way was up and which was down. It was worse than I'd thought it would be, but at the same time strangely exhilarating knowing you'd faced your fears and come out the other side. Tom whooped next to me. I'd come to a fairground with a masochist. My life choices definitely needed to be examined.

Finally, the ride came to a stop and the same man who'd fastened us in released us. If it wasn't for his long, bushy black beard, I would have been tempted to kiss him from the sheer joy of being alive. On slightly shaky legs—at least mine were, Tom's were probably fine—we made our way through the barriers toward the exit.

Once there, I leaned against the fence, cataloguing each limb separately until I was able to confirm that they were all still attached. Tom nudged my shoulder with his and held his hand up in the air. "I think you broke it."

Oh fuck! I'd completely forgotten holding on to it throughout the ride. Now that I thought about it, I did have a vague memory of squeezing it pretty damn hard. "I'm so sorry."

He shuffled forward until our chests were pressed together, his hand still between us. "You could kiss it better."

It must have been the adrenaline still coursing through my system that made me take hold of it. I gently removed his glove, turning his hand over so that it was palm up. Lifting it to my mouth, I dropped a kiss on the soft skin, our gazes meeting as my lips made contact. Tom appeared dumbstruck. He obviously hadn't expected me to do it. Common sense started to trickle back in. I was giving him the wrong message. Less than ten minutes ago, I'd resolved never to see him again. Now I was kissing his hand. What the fuck was wrong with me? I busied myself with tucking his fingers back into his glove, attempting to prolong the moment before I'd have to look at him.

"Aiden, I—"

Salvation came in the unlikely form of a traveling circus troupe. I grabbed Tom's arm and spun him round, cutting short whatever words he'd been about to say that I probably didn't want to hear. "Look." As an excuse to break the tension generated by my absurdly tender gesture, it was perfect.

Tom did look, taking in the juggling unicyclist who led the small group. They were followed by an ornately dressed king and queen on stilts, who waved to the crowds as they passed by, and Tom insisted on having his picture taken with them. I didn't mind, even if it meant I had to remove my gloves in order to be able to operate the phone camera. It was a small price to pay to break the bubbling sexual tension that had been present between us. Once they were out of sight, I immediately launched into a conversation in the hope that he'd forget altogether what had been happening before the distraction. "What next?"

"Your turn to choose a ride."

I smirked, already planning my revenge. "You said we were going to go on all of the rides, right?"

He nodded, but it soon turned into a headshake as I started to pull him toward the carousel. He tried to plant his heels but I was stronger. "I meant the adult ones."

"It is an adult one. Look, there're adults on it." There were. I wasn't making it up. The fact that most of them were accompanied by children had nothing to do with it as far as I was concerned. Tom had no choice but to grudgingly agree, his grumpy face as he perched on the back of a reindeer—it was, after all, a Christmas carousel—making me laugh. As retribution went, it was fairly satisfying. I decided right then, the scarier the ride he took me on, the more kids' rides I was going to insist he accompanied me on.

For the next hour we worked our way around the rides. I had to admit that Tom had been right, everything else, even the roller coasters, paled into insignificance after the horror of the first ride. From rides we moved on to food and games, Tom insisting on sampling everything from waffles to Halloumi fries. Seeing as he insisted on paying for everything, I wasn't going to argue.

As for the games, we gave up after a few, both of us discovering that we were equally as bad and had about as much chance of winning anything as we had of being elected prime minister. Then we grabbed a drink at one of the many bars, the huge firepit at its center providing some much-needed warmth. The last thing on Tom's list was to browse the stalls, neither of us feeling inclined to buy anything.

It was only as we were heading toward the exit that it dawned on me how much I'd genuinely enjoyed myself. Seeing everything through Tom's eyes, watching the way he'd lit up at each new thing he'd discovered, whether it was Santa going by on a decorated float, or spotting the tiny penguins outside the Ice Mountain, had reminded me that there was nothing wrong with taking joy in simple things. What's more, he was a world away from the seductive yet sullen man who'd sucked my cock in a pub toilet and offered his ass to me. That Tom had made me want to fuck him. This Tom made me yearn to spend more time with him. I liked him far more than I could allow myself to.

We paused at the edge of the park, the lights and noise from Winter Wonderland present, but muted. Tom stepped close, our bodies almost touching. He tipped his head back and stared up into my face. "Thank you."

For a moment, I was transfixed. In the dim light, he was all angles and pale skin, the only dash of color a touch of red on his cheekbones and nose where the cold had chapped the skin. Long eyelashes framed his pretty blue eyes. *Eighteen. Don't touch.* I managed to focus on his words. "For what?"

His lips curved into one of the genuine smiles I'd begun to crave. "Many things. Agreeing to come in the first place. Going on rides you didn't want to so that I could. Finishing off everything I couldn't eat. I've had such a good time tonight."

I needed to look away from him but I couldn't. *Eighteen.* "Me too."

The air between us grew static, thickening by the second. He moved closer so that our chests touched. I could feel his body warmth even through the thick layers of both of our coats. "I want to thank you properly."

"You don't need to. It's not necessary." My voice sounded unnaturally husky. Like I was aroused. Hell, who was I trying to kid? I *was* aroused. *Eighteen. Leave him alone.*

Something cold and wet landed on my forehead causing me to lift my gaze to the sky. It was snowing, the first snow of the year. That first snowflake was followed by another, a larger one, this one landing on my nose. And then there were more. It should have had us rushing for the tube station. London was notorious for grinding to a halt at the merest hint of snow.

At the moment, though, I couldn't bring myself to care about the vagaries of London's transport system. There was only Tom and the expression of wonder on his face at the fact that it was snowing. Tom and his body heat, Tom and his plump lips, so close to mine, begging to be kissed. We'd been naked together. Frotted until we both came. I'd come in his mouth. But we'd never kissed.

Eighteen. Eighteen. Eighteen. I wasn't sure when our faces had gotten so close. Had he moved? Or had I? I didn't suppose the who and the how really mattered. Only the fact that we were sharing the same breath. Tom's hands moved to rest on my chest, his fingers curling around the lapels of my coat. His eyelashes fluttered closed as if the kiss was a foregone conclusion. Snowflakes landed on his closed eyelids, making me want to strip my gloves off and brush them away.

Instead though, I closed the gap, my cold lips brushing his. At first it was just an exploratory caress, a "may I" sort of touch? Even though his permission was already implicit in everything from his tipped-up face to the fact that he was pressed close. Then his lips parted and I fell into the kiss, needing more, needing to taste, needing to give in and experience everything he had to give. Even though we were already pressed together, I found myself attempting to pull him closer.

It was a cliché to say he tasted sweet, but he did. The taste of the maple syrup from the waffles still clung to his tongue as I explored it with mine. Lips that had previously been cold slowly heated, a startling contrast to the tiny pinpricks of cold snow that continued to fall.

And still I needed more. Knocking his hat off, I buried my fingers into his thick, dark hair, berating the fact that I was wearing gloves and couldn't feel it properly. I needed to feel; my senses screaming out for it. I tilted his head, deepening the kiss. As first kisses went, it was mind-blowing, a perfection I couldn't remember ever encountering before and couldn't envisage experiencing again with anyone else. I lost track of time as we kissed. It could have been anything between one minute and ten. But every second it continued, I felt as if I discovered something new about him. The way he kissed; the noises he made; the way he gave it his wholehearted focus.

When we finally separated, I was left disorientated. Feeling like I didn't even know where I was. At some point the snow had started falling harder, the few flakes turning into a flurry. I crouched to pick up Tom's hat, brushing the worst of the snow that had settled off it before standing and sheepishly offering it back to him. "Sorry."

He took it but made no move to place it back on his head. "You better not be apologizing for kissing me."

Was I? I didn't know what I was apologizing for. Maybe for the fact that I felt like I was leading him on. Not having the words to explain, I simply shrugged.

"I should have kissed you in the pub toilet."

I couldn't help myself. "Before or after you sucked my dick?"

Thankfully, Tom didn't seem to take it as an insult, amusement lurking in his eyes, discernible even in the dim light. "Before *and* after. And probably during as well."

"Maybe." The word hung between us, both of us seeming at a complete loss as to what to say next. I focused on watching the snow settle.

"When can I see you again?"

Such a simple question. But it had as much impact on my psyche as a long thought-out speech would have done. I'd convinced myself that seeing him was okay when we were just friends. But that kiss. That soul-destroying, I-want-to-do-it-again-and-again kiss had shown me the truth. I couldn't be friends with Tom. No matter how lonely he might be and how desperately he needed one. Not now that I'd had a proper taste. Especially when he made no secret of the fact that he wanted more. To spend time with him was to fight temptation until I inevitably gave in.

"Aiden?"

I'd been so lost in my own thoughts, I hadn't answered. "You can't. *We* can't."

His eyebrow arched. "What?"

"It's not a good idea."

He rocked back as if I'd physically struck him, his face tightening. I hated doing this. But it was better to do it now rather than later. Better to nip this thing in the bud than to give him false hope of something that could never work.

"Why?" His face turned belligerent. "And don't give me all that crap about age. What the fuck does it matter if there's a bit of an age gap between us?"

"You're a virgin." Perhaps it was unfair to throw that back at him. But it was certainly valid. At least in my mind. Deflowering virgins wasn't what I did. It had only happened the once as far as I knew and that was because I was seventeen years old and one myself. It had been a mutual deflowering.

"Which you didn't even know until I told you." Tom's eyes flashed with barely concealed anger. "I should have kept my mouth shut and you'd have been none the wiser. Also, if that's such an issue, it's easily solved. I'm sure I can find someone willing to help me out if you're so reticent."

"Don't do that!" The words were out before I could stop them. "It should be with someone special. Someone your own age who means something to you. Not some stranger you've picked up as if your first time means nothing."

"*You* mean something to me."

The words were almost a plea, making me feel like the biggest dick who'd ever walked the planet. I'd brought this on myself by kissing him. Who wouldn't take that as encouragement? I'd known that but I'd still done it. I attempted one more convincing argument, hoping to undo some of the damage I'd just wrought with my selfish actions. "It's not just the age thing. We're completely different people. Complete opposites of the spectrum. Miles apart in terms of everything, really."

The lips I could still taste twisted into a sneer. "I'm not sure who you're making excuses to. Me or yourself. You want me. I know you do. You wanted me from the moment you first saw me. That's why I came over to you. I was leaving. Going home. But no one's ever looked at me the way you did before. So I had no choice but to approach you. And that kiss we shared. That kiss was..." He shook his head and let out a humorless laugh before jamming his hat back onto his head, the snow around us, now a swirling blizzard.

Then, without another word, he turned on his heel and stalked off in the direction of the tube station. I'd gotten what I'd wanted. Tom accepting that we weren't going to happen, so why did it feel like such a hollow victory? I followed his path, walking slowly, my steps weighed down by regret.

Chapter Seven

I wouldn't say it was warm in the house we were refurbishing, given the lack of an external door. But it was a damn sight warmer than outside, especially when you were wielding a sledgehammer as I was. It was just a shame that the rubble from the connecting wall I was demolishing needed to be constantly transported outside to the skip. I swung the sledgehammer again at the plaster, pausing to wipe the dust off my brow as the wall obediently crumbled under the onslaught.

Picking the chunks up with my gloved hands, I tossed them into the now-full wheelbarrow, hoping someone else might offer to take it outside. No one did of course. *Bastards.* Which left me with the option of taking it out myself or being a complete ass and pulling rank. The second option was tempting, considering the snow was at least a foot deep outside. It had started snowing three days ago when I'd been in Hyde Park with Tom and didn't feel like it had stopped for more than five minutes since.

JT appeared in the open doorway, his bulk filling it. "Hey, ugly. Your boyfriend's outside. He's asking to see you."

"I don't have a..." That was as far as I got before realization dawned as to who he must be referring to. Tom. It had to be. Three days and I'd heard nothing from him. No phone calls. No messages. Nothing. I wouldn't go so far as to say I was disappointed but I'd certainly found it surprising, given how persistent he'd been up to that point. I internally cursed the fact that I'd let the location of my workplace slip during one of the Winter Wonderland conversations. But how could I have known he'd turn up here?

"Want me to tell him you're busy?"

I shook my head. I'd already been a dick to Tom. What with the whole kissing him and then rejecting him less than five minutes later. There was no reason to compound it further. The least I could do was find out what he wanted. And if he was still operating under the delusion that something might happen between us, then I would politely but firmly repeat what I'd said to him before. Grabbing the handles of the wheelbarrow, I heaved it up onto its front wheel. Son of a bitch weighed a ton. Either that or I was getting old. "I've got to take this outside anyway. I'll see what he wants while I'm out there." I paused as I drew level with JT. "And for the record, he's not my boyfriend."

He smirked. "Sure, he's not. Everyone's casual fling turns up at their workplace with a Christmas present for them."

"A Christmas present?"

He nodded, the smirk still in place. "Hey, what do you think it is? Something horrifically expensive? Reckon he's bought you a matching Rolex? If so, you wanna hang on to that one."

"You're not funny." I shoved past him, JT only just managing to leap out of the way before I ran over his foot with the wheelbarrow.

I dumped the load of rubble in the skip before turning and scanning the yard. It didn't take long to spot him. He was standing over by the perimeter fence. When he saw me looking his way, he raised a gloved hand to wave, the other—just as JT had said—holding a brightly wrapped box with a bow on top.

Sighing heavily, I inclined my head toward the mobile cabin a few feet away, praying it was empty. It ought to be at this time, unless someone had sneaked in there for an extra break. There was no way I was going to talk to Tom outside though, no matter how brief the conversation was going to be. He might be dressed for the elements in a hat, scarf, gloves, and long coat, but I wasn't.

I waited until he'd started to walk in that direction before ducking inside the small cabin. It *was* empty, thank God. There was no way I needed an audience. I was already going to get enough flak later on just from Tom turning up here.

Tom's tailored perfection when he stepped inside made me all the more aware of what a mess I must have looked: a mixture of sweat, dirt, and dust clinging to me. Yet another reminder—not that I needed one—of the startling differences between the two of us. "What do you want, Tom?"

He smiled and held out the box, the bright paper glinting in the light. "I brought you a Christmas present."

I made no move to reach out and take it from him, eyeing it warily and wondering what it might contain, unable to get that bloody Rolex JT had joked about out of my head. What if it was something like that? "Why?"

The smile didn't shift. "It's what people do at Christmas. Give each other gifts. Don't worry, I'm not expecting anything in return." He held it out farther. "Here."

I had no choice but to take it. I grasped it gingerly and then squeezed it onto the only corner of the table not covered in dirty mugs, most of them looking more like a science experiment gone wrong than dishes to be washed. We only tackled them when we completely ran out, and even then we drew straws for the job no one wanted. "Thanks."

Tom shuffled uncomfortably on the spot. "It's not the only reason I'm here."

I let my raised eyebrow do the talking.

He sighed. "I thought you might have reconsidered. You know, absence makes the heart grow fonder and all that."

"I haven't."

He nodded, a muscle in his cheek twitching. "Right."

I expected him to leave but he stayed where he was. An awkward silence stretched between us until I felt forced to break it. "I'm not something you can add to your collection."

His eyebrows knit together. "What's that supposed to mean?"

It had been a stupid thing to say but now I'd backed myself into a corner where I had no choice but to elaborate. "I get that it's hard for you when you find something you can't have. You've got the big house. The money. You don't have to work. You've got everything."

"Is that right?"

If I hadn't been able to tell from the expression of fury on his face that I'd struck a nerve, then the cold tone he'd delivered the question in would have been a giveaway. He took a step toward me and I instinctively took a step back in the face of such antagonism. "You think I have everything?"

"Well, don't you?"

One of the site apprentices popped his head through the door, took one look at Tom's face, and decided against coming in. I couldn't say I blamed him.

Tom raised a hand in the air, his fingers trembling. "I'll tell you about my life, shall I? I'm an only child. Know why?"

I shook my head, knowing it was a rhetorical question anyway when there was no way I could possibly know the answer.

"Because my parents never wanted kids. I was an errant sperm who managed to get through a split in the condom. And I know that because my mother's told me several times. I've no idea why she went ahead and had me. Maybe an abortion was too distasteful for her. Or she couldn't fit it in between lunch dates. Who knows? So in the end she decided it was easier to go ahead and have the kid and then palm it off onto a nanny. A nanny, I might add, who was the closest thing I had to a mother. At least until her services were no longer required on my fifteenth birthday." A look of sorrow crossed his face before he continued.

"Then I was pretty much left to my own devices. They didn't even notice if I stayed out all night. That night I ended up in the gutter, it wasn't just my so-called friends that didn't give a toss. My own parents didn't either. I can't tell you how many times I came home high as a kite or completely pissed. Sometimes I think I only did it to try and get a reaction out of them. Did they say one word to me? I'll tell you the answer in case you haven't already guessed it. No, they didn't. They didn't give a damn."

Each little tidbit of pain he tossed out cut into me that little bit deeper. And still he wasn't finished. It was like now that he'd started being honest, he didn't know how to stop himself.

"I tried to make friends once. Normal friends, not ones who wanted me to buy drugs for them. Do you know what happened, Aiden?"

I shook my head again.

"They were like you. They thought we were too different. That our worlds were too far apart. Just like you, they made that judgment without bothering to get to know me." For a moment he stood silently in the middle of the mobile cabin, appearing impossibly lost and forlorn. "Yes, I have money. But that's it. That's all I've got. And I've learnt the hard way that money doesn't buy love. If anything, it drives people away."

I didn't know what to say. Even with Tom looking at me expectantly, waiting, I couldn't dredge up anything that seemed remotely suitable. I could say sorry, but that one word seemed so lacking given the length and intensity of his speech that it was almost worse than saying nothing. He was right. I had judged him unfairly. All this time, I'd been worrying about him looking down on me, and it wasn't him who'd been prejudiced. It was me. But how was I supposed to put that into words?

He laughed, his gaze dropping to the floor. "Merry Christmas, Aiden. I hope you like your present."

Then, just as he had in Hyde Park, he turned and left. For a few frozen seconds I stood there before forcing my body into motion and following. JT was leaning casually against the wall of the cabin, my coat dangling from his finger. "I'm assuming you're going to go after him. If so, you're going to need this."

I snatched my coat from his grasp, struggling to shove my arms into the sleeves as I watched the back of Tom's head disappear off into the distance. "Were you listening to the whole conversation?"

JT shrugged. "Not the whole conversation, no. Mainly the raised voice bits because they were much easier to make out." He slapped me on the back. "Now go! You've at the very least got some apologies to make. I'll cover for you if anyone notices you're missing."

I nodded my thanks and hurried after Tom, who by this time was almost at the end of the street. It was lucky that my strides covered a lot more ground than his did, meaning it didn't take me too long to close the gap. "Tom." He either hadn't heard or more likely was choosing to ignore me. I tried again louder. Same result, even though I was closer. "Tom, please stop. I need to talk to you."

He stopped dead and slowly turned around. The fact that he had tears streaming down his face shook me to the core. "I'm sorry. I didn't mean to make you cry."

He dashed at his face with his gloved palm. "*You* didn't make me cry. I guess I'm just feeling sorry for myself. That's all. Nothing to do with you." He gesticulated back in the direction we'd both come. "You can go back to work. Apologize to your workmates for me, would you? Tell them that I'm only eighteen, so you know, it's what eighteen-year-olds do... throw childish tantrums. Tell them I'll probably grow out of it one day."

I let out a sigh, wondering when we'd gotten to the point of sniping at each other like a married couple. "I shouldn't have judged you. You were right about that. I have no idea what your life is like. I made some ridiculous assumptions based on very little due to my prejudices about rich people. I was wrong and I can't apologize enough for that."

More tears leaked from his eyes. "Don't be nice to me."

"Sorry."

"And stop saying sorry."

"Sorry."

We both laughed, except his was more of a hiccup. I gave in to what I'd wanted to do ever since I'd realized he was crying: I pulled him into my arms, his head tucking under my chin perfectly. Fastening my arms around him, I held on tight.

His voice was muffled, coming as it did from my coat. "What are you doing?"

"Trying to make you feel better and stop both of us from freezing to death at the same time."

"Okay."

We stood like that for over a minute, neither of us in any rush to move apart.

"Aiden?"

"Yeah."

"I wish you could get over your hang-ups."

"Which ones in particular?"

"Age and wealth."

I wanted to say I was over them. But was I? I didn't want to lie to him. Not when I'd already forced him into talking about things he wasn't comfortable with. Not to mention making him cry, no matter how much he might deny that I'd been the cause. If nothing else, I'd certainly been the catalyst. Instead I just made a noise.

He tipped his head back so he could stare up into my face. "Kiss me."

I stared solemnly back at him. "I'm all dusty."

He arched an eyebrow. "Let me guess, you're going to tell me to find someone clean to kiss. You're all dusty. I'm all blotchy and teary. We're a perfect pair."

I cupped his face, swiping my thumb under one eye to collect the moisture that still remained there before doing the same to the other. "You're gorgeous."

"Kiss me, then."

There was no fighting it anymore. My willpower had disappeared at some point when I'd left work to chase him down the road because I cared. Not just because I'd upset him but because I cared about *him*. The man that lay beneath all the complex layers. The layers that made him seductive, intriguing, and adorable, all at the same time.

I dipped my head, joining my lips with his as Tom's arms wound around my neck, his fingers sinking into my hair. We might have been back to kissing in the snow, but this kiss was very different to our first. There was no gentle exploration needed when we both knew exactly what the other desired. Just unbridled enthusiasm on both our parts, our lips and tongues seeking a reunion. I held him tightly, resenting all the thick clothing that kept getting between us. He went to draw back and I didn't let him, chasing his lips to prolong the kiss.

I was ready to admit it. I loved kissing him. But I'd be lying if I said it didn't make me recall the other stuff we'd done: the blow job; the fact that I'd had him stripped naked and had come so close to fucking him without realizing I'd be taking his virginity; our mutual orgasm when we'd frotted together until we both came. It was all there in the kiss, and I suddenly hated that we'd done everything backwards.

Finally, I eased away from him, releasing his lips but keeping him in my arms. "What are you doing for Christmas?" It was only three days away.

His face shadowed. "Nothing, probably. I expect my parents will be in New York. Or Paris. Or Rome. Or some combination of the three."

"Will you go with them?"

He shook his head. "I won't be invited. I doubt they'll even bother to tell me they're leaving. It's just the way it is. I'll probably..." He stepped back and I let him go, already missing his warmth. He stared off into the distance. "I don't know. Watch TV or something. It's only one day. I'll pretend it's nothing special. That's what I usually do." He forced a smile. "It's always worked up to now."

As a coping strategy, it really sucked. It made me simultaneously sad and angry that his parents could treat him like that. Now that I knew his backstory, it was easy to understand why he seemed older than eighteen. I guess you grew up fast when you were left on your own. It was also easy to understand the roots of the perpetual air of cynicism he wore. "You could..." I paused, feeling stupid.

"I could what?" His eyes were intent on my face.

What was the worst that could happen? He could laugh at me and tell me where to stick my offer. At least he'd have an offer. "My sister and my niece are coming over for Christmas dinner. Nothing fancy. Just, you know, turkey and the trimmings. You could join us if you want? Or, they're usually gone by four. If you don't feel comfortable coming for dinner, you could come later."

Tom scuffed his feet into the snow. "I don't need a pity invitation."

"It's not. I promise. I can not want you to be alone without it being pity. I'll text you my address."

I waited while he processed his thoughts. He tipped his head to one side, and suddenly the Tom from the pub bathroom was back, the gleam in his eye unmistakable. "You do realize that if you let me into your house, I'm going to do my utmost to get you into bed? I might be able to hold off while your sister's there. But after that, I'm making no promises."

Heat surged into my cheeks as well as a lower part of my anatomy. "I'd be disappointed if you didn't."

He smiled wickedly. "And what are my chances of success?"

My heart began to pound. "I'd say fifty-fifty."

"Fifty-fifty!" He winked. "I'll take those odds. They're considerably better than they were before. They're 'I'll bring condoms' odds." He glanced around to check if anyone was watching before stepping forward, his hand cupping my cock through my jeans and smiling smugly at the fact that I was well on my way to being hard. "Oh yeah, I'm definitely bringing condoms."

He gave my dick one last squeeze before taking a step back, his eyes never leaving my face. "I better let you get back to work. I'll see you on Christmas Day."

I nodded, even the word goodbye sticking in my throat. He was eighteen and I didn't give a flying fuck anymore. He was just Tom. Tom, who made me feel alive and had somehow wormed his way past all my defenses.

Chapter Eight

A furrow appeared on my sister, Anabelle's brow as I slid my phone back into my pocket. "Are you going to keep checking that every five minutes?"

I scowled at her. "Hardly every five minutes. That's a slight exaggeration."

A wail broke out as my baby niece, Grace, who was propped up on the sofa, tipped sideways, only to be righted by my sister's lightning-fast reflexes before she could fall on her face. "Just about. You checked it all the way through dinner."

I probably had. I'd been so sure that Tom would turn up, and when he hadn't, I'd expected a call or a message or something. But there'd been nothing; my phone stayed deafeningly silent no matter how many times I'd squinted at the screen. It bothered me. Not just because he wasn't here but because I hated to think of him rattling around in that huge house with no one to talk to, alone and miserable.

But then, I guess if he was that miserable, he would have shown up. Maybe he was waiting for my sister to leave. It would hardly be surprising if he wasn't up for meeting extended family when we'd barely worked out what our relationship was ourselves, never mind been expected to put a label on it for someone else. What would I have introduced him as? My friend? My boyfriend? I wasn't sure, so perhaps it was just as well he wasn't here. What time had I told him my sister would have left by? Four? I checked my watch. It was just gone three. There was still plenty of time.

"Oh my God! Now you're checking your watch as well. What's going on, Aiden?"

I regarded my sister silently for a few seconds, weighing up the pros and cons of telling her. She might be younger than me by three years but she wasn't above turning the thumbscrews to extract information. It was easier to give in. "I sort of invited someone to come for dinner today."

Anabelle's eyebrows rose. "Sort of? What does that mean? You either did or you didn't invite them. There's no sort of."

I shrugged, pretending a casualness I was far from feeling. "Okay. I did invite them, then."

Her expression was one of stunned shock. "On Christmas Day? I didn't even know you were seeing anyone. Never mind that it was serious enough to want to share Christmas with them. You've been holding out on me, brother dear." Her lips curled into a smile. "Well, I guess that explains a few things."

"What things?"

She smirked. "The plated-up Christmas dinner in the kitchen for a start. I thought you'd finally discovered the world of keeping something for the next day. I should have known better really. And"—Anabelle leaned her head in the direction of the corner of my room where my rather small Christmas tree stood on a table—"the mystery present that you haven't opened yet."

I followed her gaze to the box Tom had brought to the building site, its contents still a mystery. It hadn't seemed right to open it without him there. To be honest, I'd been surprised Anabelle hadn't given me the third degree about it earlier when we'd opened all the other presents and I'd deliberately left that one.

"Who is he?"

My mouth went dry and I realized too late that I hadn't bothered to correct her assumption that I was seeing someone. Were we seeing each other? I didn't know anymore. His absence would seem to say perhaps not.

Anabelle pulled Grace onto her knee and jiggled her up and down a few times. "Uncle Aiden is keeping secrets. That means that Uncle Aiden has got something to hide."

Heat bloomed in my cheeks. "Uncle Aiden is..." Fuck! There was no way I was going to refer to myself in the third person. "I'm not trying to hide stuff. I'm trying to think of how to phrase something delicately. Something that might..." *Shock? Surprise?* I didn't know which word to use so I ended up mumbling something incomprehensible instead. Hoping my sister wouldn't notice the unfinished sentence, I reached out, letting Grace wrap her pudgy fist around my finger and then I bit the bullet and went for it. "He's eighteen."

Going by the way Anabelle's eyes went as wide as saucers, it was a good thing she was sitting down. She opened her mouth and then closed it again without any words coming out.

"*Just* eighteen." *Fuck! Why had I added that?* "He was eighteen when I met him though." Great. Now, I'd given away the fact that I'd only known him for about five minutes. I was digging myself a deeper hole by the second. No wonder Anabelle was staring at me like she was wondering whether I'd been possessed by a demon. "And we're not seeing each other. Not really. I invited him because he was going to be alone today and that made me sad. End of story. No big deal."

"So, you and this... eighteen-year-old aren't even dating?" Anabelle placed her hands over her daughter's ears. "You're just fucking him? That's worse." She shook her head as if the information was too much for her brain to cope with. "I hope you know what you're doing, Aiden. That's all."

That made two of us.

We lapsed into silence until I let out a sigh. "Anyway, he hasn't turned up, so..."

• • ◦fo • •

FOUR O'CLOCK CAME AND went with Anabelle departing to put Grace to bed, and there was still no sign of Tom. I gave in and sent a text to him, agonizing over the exact wording for a ridiculously long period of time. In the end I went with, "*Hey, just wanted to check that you were okay?*"

No response. My phone stayed as silent as it had been all day. I guessed he'd found something better to do. It should have come as a relief. Now I didn't have to try and make any sort of decision about whether I was going to end up in bed with him. I didn't feel relieved though. After ten minutes of staring sightlessly at the wrapped gift Tom had given me, I tackled the washing up that hadn't seemed right to do when I had guests. My mind, though, was never far from Tom. Where was he? What was he doing? With whom? Had he found someone else in the last few days since I'd last seen him? Had I fallen hook, line, and sinker for all his sincerity and it had been nothing more than youthful verve until something better came along?

Finally, when I couldn't take driving myself crazy any longer and all the dishes were washed, dried, and put away, I flicked the TV on, watching a film I'd already seen twice before.

It was past seven by the time the knock sounded at the door. Switching the TV off, I did my best not to jump to conclusions as I walked to answer it. It was Christmas Day though. Who else could it be? On any other day I would have laid bets on it being JT. But even he couldn't get away with a sneaky trip to the pub on Christmas Day. Not without risking his small but feisty wife refusing to talk to him for two weeks anyway.

I was unable to hold back my grin at the sight of Tom as I opened the door. He'd come after all. In my euphoria at seeing him again, it took a moment to register all the things wrong with his appearance. Firstly, the lack of his customary hat, scarf, and gloves to brave the freezing weather conditions. He wore a coat but it wasn't even fastened, revealing only a T-shirt underneath. Definitely not adequate protection for the fact that it was the first white Christmas in years, and still snowing.

The second thing I noticed was the slight sway to his movements and the unsteadiness in his gait. It seemed to be taking all of his concentration to stay on his feet. The stench of alcohol hit me as he spoke. "I'm quite drunk." He laughed, managing to make even that sound slurred. Tom leaned heavily against the doorjamb, his eyes glazed and unfocused. "Actually, scrap the quite and replace it with very. I am very, very drunk."

I didn't know what to say. In all the scenarios I'd dreamed up about today, none of them had included him turning up absolutely trashed. He fished about in his pocket with an intense look of concentration on his face before pulling his phone out and holding it up. "I was going to stay away today. But then you messaged. I'm not okay, Aiden. Not really. " His blue eyes filled with tears. "I should probably go. Coming here was a mistake."

His words, or maybe it was the fact that he was about to cry, spurred me into action. I grabbed his arm before he could do something stupid like disappear and dragged him inside. "Don't go. You're here now."

Tom stumbled against my chest and I automatically wrapped my arms around him, pushing the door shut with my foot. I held him tight, trying to force some warmth into his freezing cold limbs. I assumed he'd gotten a cab. But he was far too cold to have only been outside for a few minutes. What had he been doing? Wandering around trying to decide whether to knock on the door or not? Tom turned his head so it fitted perfectly into the curve of my shoulder and wrapped his arms around my waist. A strange sense of peace settled over me, calming the restlessness that I could now admit had been an issue all day. He let out another laugh. "You were meant to be overcome with lust for me today. That was the plan. I was going to do my hair and turn up in tight clothes. And you were meant to find me irresistible and pounce on me."

I cupped the back of his head, stroking my fingers through the dark locks, surprised by the surge of protectiveness I felt. I breathed him in, the scent of him still there beneath the much stronger alcohol fumes. "What happened to the plan?"

His lengthy exhale tickled my neck. "My dad has this bottle of whisky that I'm not allowed to touch. Real vintage stuff. I touched it." A little giggle escaped his mouth. "I touched it so much that I drank it."

"All of it?" In my head, I was already trying to work out the logistics of taking someone to get their stomach pumped on Christmas Day.

He shook his head, his cheek brushing against my chest and making my skin tingle. "No, about half of it. I stopped when I got your message." He paused, his face burrowing farther into my chest. "I feel sick."

I started to steer him toward the bathroom. Being sick was probably the best thing that could happen. It would rid him of any alcohol that hadn't already been absorbed. I wasn't about to stick my fingers down his throat though. As it turned out, he didn't need any encouragement at all, the mere sight of the toilet triggered him to push away from me, take the few steps needed to kneel in front of it, and empty his stomach into the porcelain below. It left me standing like a lemon, unsure of what the policy was when your boyfriend/houseguest was throwing up after drinking too much. Leave him to it? Stand and wait until he'd finished like some weird sort of vomiting voyeur? Stroke his hair?

I hovered in indecision for a few moments, only making my mind up when a small, wretched sob came from the figure still hunched over the toilet. I crouched down next to him, settling for rubbing his back in soothing patterns. "Hey, don't cry. You'll feel better now that you've been sick. It's all good. Really it is."

Heaving him to his feet, I flushed the toilet before propping him up against the bathroom sink where I filled a glass with water and pushed it into his hand. "Drink this." He did as he was told, finishing the whole glass. I refilled it and encouraged him to drink that one as well. No doubt he was going to have a stinker of a hangover so it was best to try and force some liquid into him while I could.

I got a spare toothbrush out of the bathroom cabinet, unwrapping it from the packaging and covering it in toothpaste before handing it over. What followed was the messiest tooth brushing I'd ever had the misfortune to witness, with half of the toothpaste ending up on the floor or the wall. I guessed there were some things it was better not to attempt while drunk. Lesson learnt. At least Tom smelled more of mint than alcohol now though.

Divesting him of his coat, I led him over to the sofa, pushing him down and attempting to maneuver him until he took the hint that I wanted him to lie down. He curled up on his side, his eyes focused on my face. "I'm so sorry."

I tugged one of his shoes off before doing the same to the other. I assumed the apology was for turning up on my doorstep drunk. "You don't need to apologize. It's fine."

Tom rolled his head to the side. "Everyone loves a drunk visitor who throws up in their toilet on Christmas Day."

I smiled at him. "Well, I was kind of bored. So you solved that at least."

"I should go." He made a half-hearted attempt to sit up, clearly not having registered the fact that I'd removed his shoes.

I planted my hand in the middle of his chest and pushed him back down. "No, you don't. Here's what's going to happen. You're going to sleep for a couple of hours. Then, when you wake up, you'll be sober and we can talk about why drinking half a bottle of whisky isn't a good idea." I brushed his hair back off his brow in an effort to soften my words.

"You're bossy."

I gave him a mock glare. "Only when I need to be. Now go to sleep."

As his eyelids fluttered closed, I stood. I'd barely taken two steps in the direction of the door when he opened his eyes again. "Where are you going?"

His drunken befuddlement was strangely endearing. There was a part of me that knew I should be irritated by him turning up in this state. But I wasn't. He was vulnerable. Far more vulnerable than he'd come across as when I'd first met him. All I wanted to do was wrap him up and keep him safe. "I'm going to go and get the duvet to cover you with and then I'm coming straight back."

"Promise?"

"I promise."

By the time I got back, he was already asleep, stirring but not waking as I tucked the duvet in around him. I switched the lights off, the only illumination coming from the lights on the Christmas tree. For a moment I was mesmerized by the play of the multicolored lights across Tom's cheek as he slept. Smiling, I positioned myself on the floor, my back leaning on the sofa close to Tom's head. I flicked the TV on, turning the volume down low so it wouldn't disturb him, prepared to let Tom sleep for as long as he needed. After all, he was safe. He had me to look after him.

Chapter Nine

"You haven't opened my present."

I jumped at the sound of Tom's voice, having failed to realize he was awake. He'd slept for a couple of hours. Given the fact that I'd turned around and checked every five minutes that he was still breathing, he must have just woken. I twisted around so I could see his face. "Are you feeling better?"

Tom lifted his head slightly as if he was taking an inventory. "I feel a lot more sober if that's what you're asking. Head hurts though." He dropped his head back down onto the cushion. "Don't you want it?"

"The present?"

He nodded, looking sad.

I retrieved it from the other side of the room and sat back down, turning it over and over in my hands. "I was waiting for you to get here before I opened it." Yet still I made no move to do that.

"You're worried it's going to be something horrendously expensive?"

Either he could read my mind or I was just incredibly transparent. I turned it over in my hands one more time. It was very light for the size of the box. "Is it?"

A faint smile appeared on his lips. "No. It's something I made. You're probably going to laugh and then throw it away."

I picked at the corner of the paper until the edge came away, my curiosity piqued by him saying he'd made it. At least that ruled out the Rolex. "I doubt that. Things that are made mean more."

"Do they?"

I offered him a reassuring smile, noting the furrow of worry that had appeared on his brow. Whatever was in that box, I had every intention of pretending it was the most wondrous thing in the world, if only to make him feel better. As it turned out, I didn't need to pretend at all, the exquisitely made angel bringing forth genuine joy. "You made this?" I held it up to the light, admiring the craftsmanship that must have gone into it. I had no idea how you'd even start to make something like that. It was all folds of white fabric delicately painted with gold and topped off with a hand-painted face drawn with an intricate attention to detail. "It's gorgeous. I had no idea you were this talented."

He shrugged. "Art's kind of my thing."

Something clicked into place. Something that should have been obvious, had it not been for the fact that both times I'd stepped into the house in Richmond, it seemed to have addled my brain and stopped it from functioning properly. "The paintings were yours."

Tom gave a little huff of confirmation.

I wished that I'd paid more attention to them now. I remembered they were good, though. Gloomy, but good. But then, that was Tom all over. No doubt he poured all his loneliness, all his negative emotions toward his parents, onto that canvas. It made me wonder even more what could be on the paintings turned to the wall, the ones he'd stopped me from seeing. Were they even gloomier? Was that why he didn't want anyone to see them? It was on the tip of my tongue to ask, but I quashed it. Now wasn't the time.

Getting up, I replaced the angel on the tree with the new, improved one. Despite the fact that it made the rest of the tree look even shabbier, I smiled.

"You don't have to put it on the tree."

"Are you kidding?" I held up the old, battered one. If memory served me right, I'd picked it up for a couple of pounds at the market. "This one can go in the bin."

Instead of returning to the floor, I lifted Tom's feet, placing them on my lap as I squeezed onto the sofa. It was only when I rested my hand on the top that I realized how oddly domesticated it was for two people who barely knew each other. Funny how it felt so right, then. In an effort to disguise the mushy feelings floating around in my stomach, I blurted out the first thing that came into my head. "Tell me something else about you that I don't already know."

He squirmed around so that he lay on his back rather than his side, allowing us eye contact. "Like what? Another miserable story?"

I rolled my eyes at him. "Talking about you being hugely talented at art isn't miserable."

He thought for a moment. "Well, my name's not really Tom. I guess that counts as something you don't know about me."

I stared at him. "You gave me a false name?"

He laughed, wincing as the action must have caused a jolt of pain in his head. I needed to get him some painkillers, but I was loath to break the cozy atmosphere that had built up between us. The painkillers could definitely wait until he'd at least explained the name thing.

"Promise you won't laugh."

I nodded.

He let out a huff of breath. "I was christened Wentworth Rufus Thompson."

Despite my promise, my lips twitched. "Wow! That's posh."

Tom shifted himself a little higher, his feet drifting toward my crotch. I gave brief consideration to moving them but left them where they were. His lips had been wrapped around my cock so I could hardly react with outrage when his toes came into contact with the same area. He pulled a face. "Exactly. And what are you supposed to do with a name like Wentworth? You can't even shorten it to anything."

I ran possible combinations through my brain, concluding that he was right. You couldn't.

"So... I took the only part of my name I could stand and called myself that instead. My parents still call me Wentworth, but I see so little of them that it doesn't really matter. As far as I'm concerned, my name's Tom. It's just my birth certificate that disagrees."

I slipped my hand under the cover, curling it around his socked foot. On impulse, I removed the sock, grasping his bare foot and settling it more comfortably against my groin, my fingers rubbing over the bare skin. I risked a glance at him, wondering how he'd react. To my relief, he seemed amused. His smile grew as I divested the other foot of its sock, throwing it on the floor to join the first. He laughed. "Aiden Malone, do you have a foot fetish?"

"Not that I'm aware of."

He pressed down, the heel of his foot pushing against my rapidly swelling cock. Then he angled his foot so that his toes could trace the outline of my cock through my trousers. "Feels like you do."

I grabbed a hold of the unruly foot, forcing it to keep still before I could do something stupid and start using his foot as some sort of masturbatory aid. "Don't start something you're in no state to finish."

He arched a brow, but let it slip down into a more natural position. "Good point." His gaze fastened on my face. "Thanks for not hating me."

I stared at him, not even trying to hide my confusion. "Why would I hate you?"

"I stood you up, and then when I did turn up, I was ridiculously drunk and threw up. And now I'm taking up space on your sofa, trying to pretend that it doesn't feel like there's a very small man in my head, playing a very loud drum."

I smiled at the imagery. "Just because you're an idiot doesn't mean I'm going to start hating you." Something suddenly occurred to me. "Have you eaten anything today? Apart from half a bottle of whisky that is, because for the record, that doesn't count."

Tom pulled a face. "If I say no, that'll make me look like an even bigger idiot."

"But if you lie, that would be worse."

He let out a sigh. "No, then. I mean, I meant to, but I didn't quite get around to it. The whisky was more tempting. Got any toast you can spare me?"

"I can do better than that. I made you Christmas dinner. You can eat that if you want? I just need to shove it in the oven for ten minutes and warm it up."

A wide smile transformed Tom's face. "You made me dinner?"

I dipped my head, staring at the lump his feet made under the cover. "It's not a big deal. I invited you for dinner so of course I made enough for you."

"Yeah, but you saved it for me as well."

I shrugged, peeking at him from beneath my lashes, strangely embarrassed by his degree of happiness over something so simple. "Can you face it? Or do you want something lighter?"

"Christmas dinner would be lovely. Thank you. I haven't had one for years."

That flat statement of fact caused a lump to form in my throat. His parents had a lot to answer for. What the hell were they thinking? They had a fantastic son and they didn't even want to be in the same country as him for Christmas. Some people didn't deserve to have kids. I wished I'd known all of this back when I'd met his mum in the kitchen. I would have loved to give her a piece of my mind. I didn't say any of that aloud, though, as I reluctantly let go of Tom's feet and forced myself out from underneath the warmth of the cover to head to the kitchen.

I hadn't expected Tom to follow, but to be honest, the company was nice, even if it did involve both of us staring at an oven silently. I passed over a couple of painkillers, along with another glass of water which he obediently swallowed. And then we went back to staring at the oven.

"I don't want to go home."

The words resounded around my small kitchen, Tom looking almost embarrassed to have said them, as if they'd escaped from his mouth when he hadn't meant them to. "You don't have to."

"No?"

I shook my head. "You can stay here."

He leaned back out of the doorway, peering around the corner. "Place doesn't seem big enough to have a spare room."

I smiled. "It doesn't. Just the one bedroom."

He tipped his head to one side, blue eyes regarding me speculatively. "Sofa's comfy though, I guess."

It was obvious what he was implying. Only problem was I didn't know how to answer his question that wasn't really a question. Not in a way that was fully honest anyway. There were far too many feelings I still needed to quantify sloshing around inside me. I busied myself with donning oven gloves instead, pulling the reheated Christmas dinner out of the oven and covering it with the gravy I'd already heated up in the microwave before finally offering a vague response, making sure to avoid Tom's keen gaze as I did. "We'll see."

Tom turned down the offer of a seat at the table in favor of eating off a tray balanced on his knees on the sofa. To my surprise, he managed to polish it all off. I'd forgotten what a completely different beast a hangover was at eighteen to one in your thirties. I guess it had been a while since I'd had cause to think back that far. Once he'd finished, he placed the tray on the floor next to him and turned his stare my way. "You can cook. You have all those muscles, and you're good in the kitchen *and* the bedroom." He gave a wicked smile, all traces of a hangover gone. "You, Aiden Malone, might just be husband material."

While I was still struggling for an appropriate response, he dropped to his knees on the carpet. He crawled toward me, his movements deliberately slow and provocative, a seductive expression pasted on his face. My mouth went dry and I lost the ability to make words. It was amazing how quickly the vulnerable, drunken version of Tom had disappeared, the first version of him I'd met firmly in its place—the one that exuded sexual promises from every pore. My brain made an attempt to hang on to some of the blood that was heading straight to my cock. "I guess you're feeling better?"

His hands landed on my knees, pushing them apart, and I found myself looking down at him, those pretty blue eyes seductively lidded and his tongue darting out to moisten his lips. When I'd sat down, I'd automatically pulled the duvet over my lap. Tom tugged on it and I watched as it slid to the floor, baring my lower body to his gaze. And what a hot and hungry gaze it was. Enough to send my body up in flames without him doing anything else but look. He flicked his head back, dislodging the lock of hair that had fallen over one eye. "I am. Much better. Amazing what dinner and drugs can do." He smirked when he realized what he'd said. "The medicinal kind of drugs, that is. Not the sort I used to do."

Long, delicate fingers slowly travelled along my thighs, pausing every now and again to scrape along the seam of my jeans. Tom shuffled forward, his nails grazing my zipper. His intent was clear; my willpower quickly waning. I mustered an iota of self-restraint from somewhere and grabbed his wrists. I needed to be sure because I knew if I said yes, I was saying yes to far more than just a blow job. "What if you're searching for a father figure?"

Tom sat back on his haunches, amusement shining in his eyes. "Then, I'm even more fucked up than I thought because I want to suck my father figure's cock. And that's what I intend to do. At least when he stops playing so hard to get." He made an attempt to release his wrists but I held fast. "I'm serious, Tom."

His face sobered. "I'm not looking for that. I assure you that all my feelings toward you have always been one hundred percent sexual, ever since the first time you looked at me with such unbridled lust in your eyes. I don't want you to look after me, take me to the park, and buy me presents. I want you to throw me on the bed and fuck the living daylights out of me. I want you to look at me the same way you did when I stripped for you back in Richmond. Like you'd unearthed some rare treasure and you couldn't wait to get a piece of it. Does that sound like someone searching for a father figure?"

It didn't. Not one little bit. At some point during his short but passionate speech, his wrists had slipped from my grip. I wasn't sure whether I'd let go, or he'd managed to wriggle free. Only that it had left him able to continue his pursuit of my zipper. I didn't stop him as he pulled it down, his bottom lip sticking out in a way that managed to be both sexy and endearing at the same time. I didn't stop him as he undid the button of my jeans and inched them down. I still didn't stop him as he did the same with my underwear, my hard cock springing out and curling up against my still-clothed abdomen.

Tom smiled, his hand wrapping around the base of my dick. "Hello, old friend. Long time, no see."

"You're talking to my cock?"

He lifted his head, devilment dancing in his eyes. "Sure I am. Your cock's always been pleased to see me. It even shared its appreciation of my feet earlier. I have a lot of time for little Aiden. It doesn't keep questioning stuff like big Aiden does."

I slid my hand into his hair, the battle already lost. Although if I was honest, it had already been lost at the point I'd invited him to stay the night. "Your pre-sex talk is quite disturbing."

Tom relinquished his grip on my cock as he pulled his T-shirt over his head, leaving him dressed only in jeans. Then he was back, the planes of his lean chest reflecting the lights of the Christmas tree. I couldn't take my eyes off him as he pushed my thighs wider apart, insinuating himself between them. "Tell me you want me to suck your cock."

He could have asked me to say anything at that moment and I would have said it. "I want you to suck my cock."

"Tell me how badly you want it."

"I want it really badly."

His hand curled back around my shaft, my dick giving a happy little throb at the attention. Little Aiden had no qualms at all about what was about to happen. Tom's smile was a mixture of self-satisfaction and victory.

"What are you smiling at?"

"Just thinking that this is far nicer than a pub toilet. And how much of a better job I'm going to be able to do."

"Better!" *Jesus, if he did any better, then I was probably going to die from pleasure.* The previous occasion had convinced me to go home with someone I'd just met. Someone I hadn't known the first thing about. I'd discovered that to my detriment. What the hell would better get me to do? I'd be proposing marriage or asking him to move in with me.

Lips engulfing my cock put paid to any more self-analysis. I leaned my head back against the sofa as hand, tongue, and lips went to work in perfect tandem. I hated to think of why he was so good at blow jobs at such a young age, but my God, I was happy to reap the benefits.

I reached out, tracing the colored patterns of light from the Christmas tree on his skin as his head bobbed up and down, an intense look of concentration pasted on his face. He wasn't interested in making it last. His whole point of focus seemed to be on making me come as quickly as possible. And so far, he was doing a great job of it, the telltale tingle of orgasm already making itself known. He lifted his head, his hand taking the place of his mouth in a seamless transition, the teasing stroke continuing. Tom's gaze raked my face. "Are you close?"

I managed a jerky nod, words having disappeared again to that place where Tom had an unerring knack of sending them. There was only ragged breaths, broken sighs and synapses firing in my brain in every area that registered pleasure.

His lips curled into a smug smile. "Already?"

I slid down the sofa, the action pushing my cock more firmly into his hand. "Need to come." As statements of fact went, it was pretty damn obvious.

His eyes still intent on my face, Tom twisted his hand, his palm grazing the sensitive head of my cock, sending a full body shiver through me. "Do you want me to finish you with my hand or my mouth?"

I let my gaze flick between the hand keeping up the steady rhythm on my dick, and his plump lips. There wasn't any question really so I didn't even know why I was deliberating. The sight of him sucking my cock had filled my dreams ever since that first night. Much as I'd tried to fight it because of his age, it wasn't a surprise that we'd ended up right back where we'd started. "Mouth."

There was no hesitation. He got right back to it with the vigor of, I guess you'd say youth. My hips bowed off the sofa, seeking that tight moist heat that felt so damn good, only pulling back when he gagged slightly. "Sorry."

His lips formed the best smile they could when they were stretched around my cock. He pulled off. "That's alright. I don't mind a bit of enthusiasm." And then he was sliding his lips back down my cock.

I leaned back farther as the sensations grew, my eyes closing and my breath coming in harsh pants. Without sight, my other senses took over: the sound of his mouth moving over my cock ramped up my arousal even more. Tom's fingers delved beneath the sweatshirt I wore and I remembered how keen he'd been to see my chest the previous time we'd done this. Wanting to please him, I freed my hand from where it was holding on to the edge of the sofa for dear life, and pulled my sweatshirt up to my neck, baring my chest for his perusal.

My reward was twofold: a nice, husky groan around my throat-embedded cock, and deft fingers fastening on to one of my nipples and pinching. Both things together were enough to push me over the edge and I came with a shout, my abdominal muscles clenching hard enough to hurt. I kept my eyes closed, concentrating on the feel of Tom's warm tongue as he lapped at my spent dick, cleaning up any drops of cum he'd missed.

"You have very intense orgasms."

Only with you. I bit the words back, terrified of revealing too much too soon when we hadn't even come close to quantifying out relationship. I slowly opened my eyes, meeting the blue gaze of the man who'd now sucked my cock twice without me having returned the favor. It was time to rectify that. In one fluid move, I levered myself off the sofa, almost getting tangled in my jeans and underwear which had slipped to mid-calf. I quickly kicked them off before pulling Tom off the floor and pushing him down onto the sofa, a soft whoosh of breath escaping from his mouth as he landed. Then I attacked the button and the zipper on his jeans, pulling his stiff cock out and fitting it into my hand, the warm velvet flesh radiating heat.

"Take your top off."

"Huh?" I managed to pull my gaze away from where I'd been tracing a delicate vein that ran from root to tip. Back in the bedroom in Richmond, there hadn't been much opportunity to look, so I had every intention of making up for it now. Then I'd take my time tasting it as well. There were certain advantages to having come already, one being that I wasn't running on pure arousal.

Tom quirked an eyebrow at my air of distraction. "Take your top off so that I can admire those gorgeous muscles while you're busy staring at my cock."

I ran my thumb over the head, drawing a sharp intake of breath from him. "It's a very nice cock."

He smirked. "Thank you. I'm glad. It's the only one I've got. Now strip."

I ripped my sweatshirt and T-shirt over my head in one swift move, tossing them onto the floor to join the rest of my clothes. Tom's gaze ran over me—a mixture of adoration and lust reflected in the blue depths of his eyes. "Come here." He sat up as I returned to kneeling in front of him, his hands fastening on my shoulders, tracing my biceps with a light touch before moving to my pecs. "Your body is fucking perfect."

I gave him time to complete his exploration, his long fingers outlining every abdominal muscle and moving around to trace the muscles of my back before he was satisfied. He sat back with a grin, his cock leaving a fine trail of pre-cum where it brushed his abdomen. Of course, I had to touch, my thumb lifting it from his skin and bringing it to my mouth. It tasted like I expected Tom to taste, a mouthwatering combination of sweetness and salt. Like the best kind of aperitif before the main course.

I couldn't wait any longer. I buried my head in his crotch, sliding my lips over the warm, rigid skin and taking him as deep as I could.

"I won't last long."

I showed him through actions rather than words how little that mattered, increasing the speed of my mouth over his cock until he was a trembling, quivering wreck beneath my hands. Even when my jaw had started to ache—because not long was still long enough when you were out of practice—I didn't let up on him, his incoherent cries fueling my determination. Tom's fingers tightened in my hair, his whole body going rigid as his cock nudged my tonsils. He seemed to hang on that precipice for the longest time before I was finally rewarded by the spurt of warm fluid on my tongue. I kept him there, laving the softening flesh with my tongue as he sagged back onto the sofa, his chest rising and falling rapidly, his body drenched in sweat.

He laughed, his fingers dropping from my hair. "Shit! That was good."

Reaching over to the table, I grabbed a tissue, using it to finish the rest of the clean-up operation. Post orgasm, sprawled naked over my sofa, he looked like the most tempting sight known to man. If I'd been a photographer, I would no doubt have wanted to record the sight for posterity. Given my poor camera skills, I had to make do with leaning in and kissing him instead.

It was the lazy kiss of two men who were a good few minutes away from passion being able to stir again. But that made it all the sweeter. And he *was* sweet. There was no doubt in my mind about that. In what should have been a sleazy bathroom blow job, I'd managed to find something rare and precious. Or I guess he'd found me, really, considering the fact that had it not been for him,

I would have done no more than look. "Why were you in the pub that night so far from home?"

He tugged me forward, his arms encircling me to stroke over my back. "Does it matter?"

"I'm curious. Surely you can settle an old man's curiosity."

Tom gave me a pointed stare. "You're not old. Don't start that again. Don't spoil it."

I wasn't intending to spoil anything. But the fact that he wasn't answering what should have been a straightforward question made me even curiouser. Turning my head, I kissed his shoulder, the skin velvet-soft against my lips. "I guess it doesn't matter why we ended up in the same place."

Tom sighed. "If you must know, I was looking for someone."

"Who?"

"A guy."

"What guy?" I was interrogating him. I knew that, but that didn't mean I could stop myself.

Tom's teeth played with his lip as if he was reticent to explain more. "Just some guy I'd been talking to online for a while. He was meant to meet me there. But I guess he stood me up. Either that or he was never who he said he was, and didn't have any intention of meeting me in the first place. I never heard from him again, so it was probably the latter."

I stared at him aghast, hardly able to believe what he was admitting to. "You were going to meet a complete stranger off the internet. Are you insane? He could have been a serial killer."

Tom raised an eyebrow. "And instead, I met another stranger." He gestured down at our naked bodies plastered together. "And here we are."

"That's different."

"Is it?"

I guessed he had a point. The thought of him putting himself in possible danger because he'd been lonely stuck in my throat though. I couldn't get the image out of my mind of someone taking advantage of him. Or worse. "You need to be more careful."

"I know."

Tom's eyelids had started to droop. I decided that the lecture about internet safety could wait for another day. Besides, he was right. I wasn't exactly the best person to warn him about staying away from strangers. The word hypocrite sprang to mind. I pulled him up off the sofa, his head lolling against my shoulder. "Come on, sleepyhead."

He mumbled something into my skin that sounded like, "Where are we going?" It was hard to tell though when the words all ran into each other.

"Bed."

I managed to maneuver him in the direction needed to switch the Christmas lights off. Luckily, there was enough light from the hallway to prevent me from walking both of us into the furniture.

"I can sleep on the sofa." Those words were clearer, Tom lifting his head for just long enough to speak them.

I didn't even consider my answer. "No." It was easy. I didn't want him on the sofa. I didn't want to lie in another room, unable to sleep for thinking about him. He felt so good in my arms, all sleepy and pliable. That's where I needed him, tucked up next to me so the rhythm of his breathing could lull me to sleep. Pushing him gently into the bathroom, I roused Tom enough to do the necessary once I'd shoved the same toothbrush he'd used earlier into his hand with toothpaste already on it. *His toothbrush.* The thought shocked me with how right it sounded. Was I really starting to see some sort of future with him? He wrapped his arms around my waist and leaned his head against my chest. "Take me to bed, Aiden."

My attention had been caught by our reflection in the mirror. God, we looked good together. *Maybe it could work?* There were plenty of people in the world with successful relationships with an age gap. They didn't always fail. And it was thirteen years. It wasn't like I was old enough to be his father. We could make it work, right? As long as it was what both of us wanted. I was jumping way ahead though. One step at a time. It was just the endorphins still coursing through my body from the blow job, turning great sex into a happy-ever-after fairy tale. The morning would no doubt bring a new clarity that both of us needed.

"What are you thinking?"

I met Tom's gaze in the mirror, realizing how long I'd been staring at our reflection. "I'm thinking that if I don't get you into bed soon, you're going to fall asleep standing up." I turned him in my arms so that our naked bodies were pressed together, our clothes still lying in a pile on the living room floor. "Do you snore?" I felt his chuckle against my shoulder.

"If I do, are you going to leave me here?"

"Possibly." But I'd already started walking us toward the bedroom, my nose buried in his hair.

"I have no idea if I snore. I don't usually..."

There was no need for him to finish the sentence. It was obvious. He hadn't spent the night with anyone before. Therefore no one had ever told him whether he did or not. A warm glow of satisfaction at the fact that I was going to get to be the first suffused my body. "I guess we'll find out."

I pulled the covers back, ushering him into one side of the bed while I climbed in the other. A huge chasm of space lay between us. I didn't like it. I didn't like it one little bit. But then it seemed, neither did he. He shuffled backward until the curve of his ass nestled into my crotch, my cock starting to take an interest in the smooth flesh it fitted so well against. Wrapping my arm around his waist, I threw one of my thighs over his, leaving our bodies intimately entwined.

"Is this okay?" Tom's voice sounded unsure in the darkness, as if he expected to be pushed away, even though my actions were clearly indicating the opposite.

I nestled my face into the hair at the nape of his neck, breathing him in, his skin warm and silky everywhere we touched. "It's more than okay."

He wriggled his ass slightly. I wouldn't have expected anything less from him. I made no move to put some space between us, despite my cock swelling and the knowledge that he had to be able to feel what he was doing to me.

He let out a small sigh. "You still haven't fucked me."

Tightening my arm around his waist, I pulled him more firmly against me. "I know. And I'm not going to. Not tonight anyway. Go to sleep." It was going to happen. I knew that with the same inevitability that I knew the sun would rise in the morning and set again in the evening. The only thing I could still control was where and when. *If* had already disappeared over the horizon, never to be seen again. I wanted to be Tom's first but there was no rush. He didn't need to lose his virginity to a stranger like he'd come so close to doing back in Richmond. He could lose it to someone who genuinely cared about him and wanted to make him happy. Me. The question that remained unanswered though was what was going to happen after that.

It turned out that he did snore. At least if adorable little snorts could be counted as snoring. My last conscious thought before succumbing to sleep myself was that if I found even his snores charming, then I was so fucked.

Beyond fucked.

Chapter Ten

M orning didn't bring clarity. Instead, it brought a shirtless Tom sitting at my breakfast table, looking for all the world like he belonged there. It was all I could do not to simply stare at him and smile.

"Why are you wearing a shirt?"

I turned to find him with a seductive smile on his face, his gaze trailing slowly over the T-shirt I'd automatically thrown on when I got up.

"Because I have to cook breakfast for you." I threw the fridge door wide open, studying its contents. I was glad that with it being Christmas, I'd actually gone shopping. It meant having a choice of food to offer Tom. "I have bacon, sausages, and mushrooms. I have eggs so you can have fried or scrambled. Just don't ask for poached. I tried it once but let's just say it wasn't a success. I have beans and tomatoes. So basically I have all the workings for a full English if you fancy it?"

"Do you have caviar?"

The fridge door swung closed behind me as I turned and scrutinized his expression. It gave nothing away. "Is that... do you... no, sorry. No caviar. Erm..."

"I suppose you don't have smoked salmon either?"

I shook my head, racking my brains to recall whether there was any sort of posh food shop nearby that might stock caviar. Even if there was though, they weren't likely to be open on Boxing Day.

A bubble of laughter escaped from Tom's throat. "Ha! Your face with all the 'how am I going to feed a posh boy breakfast' panic. Relax. I don't eat caviar." He gave a shudder of distaste. "I mean, fish eggs. I've never really understood why that's a delicacy. I just couldn't resist playing up to the stereotype a bit."

I screwed up a tea towel and threw it at him. He ducked and it sailed over his head. "You gotta throw better than that, old man."

Stepping across the kitchen, I retrieved the tea towel from where it had fallen. He'd said old man more like an endearment than an insult. Tom used it the same way someone else might use darling. "So what *do* you want for breakfast seeing as I'm all out of caviar?"

Tom leaned forward, resting his head on his hand while looking pensive. "I'm a guest, right? So as long as it's something you've got, you have to do it?"

I crossed my arms, trying to work out what his angle was. "I don't know about *have to*, but I wouldn't be asking you if I didn't want you to have a choice."

He winked. "Then, it's easy. Tea, toast, and no shirt, please." He waggled his eyebrows. "That would make me very happy."

"Then..." I lifted my T-shirt over my head, leaving it draped over the back of a chair. "Your wish is my command."

We both ended up having toast. It seemed pointless cooking a fry-up for one person. Besides, I wanted to have breakfast *with* Tom, not spend the time cooking while he ate. It was nice to sit across from him and just be in the same space together, the two of us spending an inordinate amount of time staring into each other's eyes.

Tom wrapped his hands around his mug of tea. "We're spending the day together, right? Seeing as you don't have to work and I'm a lazy waster."

I gave him a stern look. "You're not a lazy waster."

He lifted his shoulders in a shrug. "We can agree to disagree. Now, how about you answer the question or I'll think you're avoiding it."

I hadn't imagined any other scenario apart from spending the day with him. "Yes. I don't know what we're going to do though. Everything's closed unless you want to go and look at half-price sofas and carpets." I glanced out the window, watching the large and continual flakes of snow fall. "And the weather's still shit."

Tom tapped his fingers on the table. "The weather's perfect for what I've got in mind."

The glint in his eyes said he wasn't too sure I was going to go for it. "Which is?"

He sat back. "What do you do when you have all this lovely snow that we don't get that often?"

I eyed him suspiciously. "I don't know. What *do* you do?"

His smile was triumphant. "Build a snowman, of course."

It was on the tip of my tongue to shoot the idea down, to point out that we were two grown adults, not children. But hadn't I done the same with Winter Wonderland? And hadn't I enjoyed it in the end, once I'd let go of all my preconceived ideas? And unlike the Tom I'd first met, he was smiling. Genuine smiles that didn't mask sadness and loneliness behind them. I wanted to keep him like that, and if it meant dropping some of my own barriers to do that, then it would still be well worth it. "Okay."

He cocked his head to the side. It was his turn to be suspicious. "I was expecting you to put up more of an argument than that."

I winked at him. "I'm a builder. It's what I do. I can see why you'd need to call an expert in. With me on the team, it won't be some piss-poor construction. It will be a snowman for people to marvel at. It will be *the* snowman. I'll have my quote to you within the next hour. I'm warning you though, I don't come cheap."

Tom hid his smile behind his mug as he took a drink. "Good thing my parents are filthy rich, then. It's about time they invested in the world of ice. I hear it's an increasingly popular market in the winter months."

We both dissolved into laughter. It seemed natural to reach across the table and thread our fingers together. "And where are we going to construct this magnificent snowman, the likes of which the world has never seen before?"

Tom curled his fingers around mine. "I was thinking Richmond Park. That way I can go home and get a change of clothes first. I'm not keen on wearing the same underwear as yesterday all day." He paused at the expression on my face, picking up on my lack of enthusiasm for the idea. "My parents aren't coming back until after the New Year. There's zero chance of you bumping into them if that's what you're worried about. And even if we did, they wouldn't give a damn."

"Your mum seemed like she cared when I saw her that night."

His face twisted, a dark expression settling on it. "That wasn't caring. That was…" He stared at the contents of his mug, swirling the liquid contents around as he seemed to struggle to come up with the right words. "…her trying to piss me off for existing. Don't forget that what she said wasn't true. You were the first man I'd ever taken back there. So her trying to get you to believe that you were just one in a line of men was pure vindictiveness. Maybe you wouldn't have run off if she'd been less of a bitch."

Maybe not. But, although only a few weeks ago, that night already seemed like another world. "It didn't matter. You found me again."

His lips twitched into a smile. "So you're up for Richmond, then?"

"One condition."

"Go on."

"I get to see your paintings. All of them. Even the ones facing the wall."

He stared at me and I wondered if I'd gone too far. I didn't have a clue what was on the canvases facing the wall, but he'd obviously done it for a reason. Perhaps he didn't even want to look at them himself. It was probably way too intrusive of me to demand to see them just because we'd shared a few blow jobs and spent the night in the same bed. "Sorry, that was..."

But Tom was already nodding. "Sure. Why not. What's the worst that could happen? You could hate them." He attempted to smile but it was tremulous at best and gone after a couple of seconds.

Great, Aiden. Way to spoil the mood. Demand to see someone's secret paintings before agreeing to grace them with your snowman-making skills, why don't you? Fantastic move there.

· · ❧ · ·

JUST AS TOM HAD SAID it would be, the house was as silent as a tomb. I followed him into the lounge, the one with the huge Christmas tree I'd spied in the dark on my first night there. It struck me how pointless the tree was when his parents weren't even there. It was like a lot of things in the house seemed to be: completely for show. Aesthetics over purpose. Tom picked a bottle up from the table and held it up to the light. "Oh, actually I drank less than half. My fraction estimating skills must have been compromised by my level of drunkenness."

I swiped it out of his hand, making my own inspection. About a third of the bottle was gone. "That's still way too much. What if you'd passed out here and then choked on your own vomit?"

Tom tilted his head to the side as he considered the notion. "Then, I guess getting rid of the Christmas tree this year would have been hampered by having to step over my dead body."

"Oh, come on. They'd care, right? If you were...?" I couldn't bring myself to add the word dead onto the end of the sentence.

He shrugged. "It'd mess their schedules up. They normally head to Morocco in January. A funeral would definitely take the wind out of their sails."

He had to be exaggerating. Or at least I hoped he was. I turned the whisky bottle around so that I could read the label, not that I'd recognize expensive whisky if I saw it. "Is your dad going to go ballistic about this?"

Tom crossed his arms. "I'll get frozen disapproval." He affected a hoity-toity upper-class voice. "Son, if you must drink whisky, please choose something that is not an eighteen-year-old Glenrothes. I shall have to replace the bottle now."

I stared at him, open-mouthed. "That's it. No concern?"

He laughed. "Doubt it. My dad's alright, though. At least he doesn't make sly digs like my mum. I guess you'd call him an absentee father. We're like ships that pass in the night. When we're in the same room, we usually manage to make polite conversation about the weather. Then he's out the door again."

I'd known that Tom didn't get along with his parents. He'd made that clear. But all these little snippets of his life coming out of his mouth were revealing an even bleaker picture. No wonder he'd been up for meeting a complete stranger off the internet. One thing was for sure, I'd been an absolute fucking idiot for believing that money was everything. My life was so much richer than Tom's in a number of ways, despite the frequency of the minus next to the numbers in my bank account when payday was approaching. "I'm sorry."

There didn't seem to be a lot else I could say. I couldn't wave a magic wand and give him a better childhood. Better parents. All I could do was try and make the present a bit more bearable. A weird, charged silence simmered between us. In an effort to dispel it, I busied myself with removing the thick coat and scarf Tom had insisted I wear. I'd already removed my hat and gloves when I'd walked in the door.

Tom sighed. "Do you want to wait here while I go and get changed?" His lips curled into that familiar seductive smile. "Or do you want to come and watch?"

I slung my coat over the back of the sofa. "Well, given that the paintings you're meant to be showing me are upstairs, then, I better come and watch."

He grinned. "Ah, right. It's the artwork you want to see, not my body. I understand."

I gave him a little shove as he headed out the door to the stairs, relieved to have moved away from the subject of his parents. "Shut up. As you very well know, I want to see both."

His room appeared exactly the same as it had the last time I'd been there. I seated myself on the edge of the bed, unable to stop my gaze from straying to the paintings propped up against the wall. Only this time, I was viewing them with completely different eyes, knowing Tom had painted them. On my previous visit, I'd barely taken notice of what the paintings were of. Now I did. Most of them were places: rolling hills and riverbanks; a deserted city street; a forest. I leaned closer to get a better look at one. I was no art expert—not even close—but even I could see that they were good, each little detail depicted carefully, the leaves on the trees in the forest all individual in size, shape, and color.

"What do you think?"

There was a nervous edge to Tom's voice. I lifted my head to find him studying me. "They're fantastic. You're very talented." I gestured at the ones facing the wall. "But I'm dying to know the secret behind those ones."

Tom walked over to the closest one, his fingers tightening around the edge of the canvas. He chewed on his lip for a moment. "These ones are of people. I wanted to branch out a bit. Challenge myself. There's two reasons they're this way around. Firstly, I don't think they're as good, and secondly, I have to sleep in here. It's a bit weird to have them all looking at me."

He hesitated for a moment before flipping the first canvas around to face me. The subject was an elderly gentleman, the background depicting a coffee shop. The startling thing was how well Tom had managed to capture the man's wistful expression. The pictures of scenery were good, but they lacked character. Whereas this painting had it in spades. You couldn't look at it without wondering what the man had been thinking about. A lost wife maybe? A family who didn't visit him anymore? Or was he simply remembering the days when he was younger?

Tom did a circuit of the room, turning the canvases around one by one to reveal an array of people: a woman caught laughing as her hat flew off on a windy day; a child struggling to hold a dog that was much bigger than he was; a young couple on a park bench staring lovingly into each other's eyes. Just like the first painting, I could tell so much about these people from the image he'd reproduced.

"You're really quiet. I'm taking that as a bad sign. I told you they weren't as good."

"I'm busy marveling."

"Marveling?" There was a hint of embarrassment in Tom's voice. "You don't have to say that."

I pulled my attention away from the paintings and back to him, needing to make eye contact so that he'd know I was sincere. "I know I don't *have* to say that. But it's the truth. The landscapes are great, but these are even better." I wished I had some sort of background knowledge to draw upon in order to be able to say the right things, but seeing as manual labor had never prepared me to talk about depth, color, and composition, that was all I could give him. My honest and unvarnished truth. He'd left one painting facing the wall. "What's on that one?"

Tom waved a dismissive hand. "Nothing important."

"Is it a guy?"

He frowned. "Why would you jump to that conclusion?"

"Because you won't show it to me. So my brain's trying to come up with plausible reasons why you'd show me the rest of the portraits but not that one."

He exhaled noisily. "If you must know, it's a self-portrait."

I circled my finger in the air, a silent instruction to spin it around. "You said I could look at all of them. Not all of the paintings apart from one." For a moment, it seemed as if he was going to argue, and then he shrugged and did as I'd asked. The painting was beautiful, but sad. In exactly the same way he'd manage to capture all his other subjects' characteristics, he'd managed to do the same with his own. It radiated loneliness, which I hadn't even realized it was possible for a painting to do before seeing this one.

I tried to work out why. The slump of his shoulders, maybe? Or the faraway look in his eyes. Or maybe it was the fact that he seemed smaller somehow than the people in the other paintings. Like the background was about to swallow him up. I didn't know. All I knew was that looking at it made me feel miserable.

As if sensing my thoughts, Tom returned it to its original position, leaving me staring at the paint-splattered, but otherwise blank, back of it. I lifted my head to look at him. "Come here." He ambled across the room, coming to a stop in front of me, the blue eyes holding a silent question. In order to exorcise the memory of the first Tom I'd met, the one immortalized on canvas, I needed to get him smiling again. Needed to remind myself that he didn't have to be lonely anymore because now he had me. "You promised me a bit of stripping. Give me something else apart from your incredible talent to marvel at."

A glint appeared in his eye. "Marvel, you say. What does that involve, exactly? Just so I can decide if it's worth it."

"A lot of appreciative looks and maybe a bit of touching."

He sucked air between his teeth and shook his head at the same time. "I don't know about the touching. Not sure that's allowed. I'm not a piece of meat, you know."

I leaned back on my elbows on the bed, giving him my best lascivious glance. "Yeah, you are. You're..." I searched around for a good enough comparison. "...fillet steak. You're lean, tender, tasty, and classy."

The smile I'd been searching for appeared on Tom's lips. He pulled his T-shirt over his head. "Is that right? What does that make you?"

"Minced beef."

He laughed, his fingers making deft work of his button and fly before pulling his jeans down and stepping out of them. "More like rump steak. Tough and sinewy, but if cooked right, just as tasty."

I'd take that comparison any day. My mouth almost started watering as Tom stepped out of his underwear, leaving him naked, and I got my first proper look at him in the daylight. He was all lean muscles and soft skin with not an ounce of fat on him. I reached out, but he immediately slapped my hand away with a grin. "No touching, remember."

Lunging to my feet, I grabbed him, pulling his nude body against my clothed one, my hands sliding down his back to cup his bare ass cheeks. I swallowed his mock protest with my mouth, Tom's response just as enthusiastic. It was only when his dick started to harden against my thigh that I considered our surroundings. I might have gotten over the stumbling block of his age, but sexual acts in his childhood bedroom were another thing entirely. I dropped one last soft kiss on his lips before pushing him gently away. "Stop trying to seduce me and get dressed. We've got a snowman to build."

Tom's mouth dropped open. "Me! Seduce you? I think you're getting things a bit mixed up there, old man. You were the one with the octopus-hands." He fluttered his eyelashes. "What's a poor innocent boy to do when he's overpowered by a giant of a man with much bigger muscles than his own?"

I laughed. "Put his clothes on so that giant of a man can think about something other than sex."

He walked over to the chest of drawers, slowly and deliberately bending over to leave his pert ass stuck straight up in the air. God, it was a sight to behold. My cock throbbed at the thought of how it might feel to bury myself in that ass. Tom glanced back over his shoulder with a knowing smile. "Oh, silly me. Wrong drawer."

I groaned. Yeah, I was fucked, and it wasn't going to be long before he was too.

Chapter Eleven

We weren't the only people in Richmond Park who'd gathered there with the intention of making a snowman. However, from what I could see, we were the only ones over the age of twelve. Tom grabbed me by the hand, muttering something about not competing for snow, and dragged me on what felt like a five-mile hike to the center of the park, where there was no one else around save for the two of us. He'd insisted on bringing a bag of what he'd termed "necessary snowman apparel" from his house, which he carefully deposited on the ground before looking around. "You do the body and I'll do the head."

I stared at him. I knew enough about making snowmen to know how much bigger the body needed to be in relation to the head. "Why do I get the difficult job?"

He arched an incredulous eyebrow. "Erm... muscles. Strength." He waggled his glove-covered fingers in the air. "I'm the artistic one, remember. I'll be in charge of all the finishing touches."

I shook my head. "This is not the job I signed up for. You're going to have to make it worth my while."

He lifted his chin. "Playing hardball, I see. Name your price."

"A kiss."

His lips quirked before he schooled them. "An unusual request but not unreasonable, I suppose."

"Every five minutes."

Tom shook his head slowly and made a clicking noise. "That's a very steep price for a big ball of snow."

"Take it or leave it."

This time, he gave in to the smile pulling at his lips. "I suppose you're expecting a deposit, aren't you? Your lot are never willing to start the work until you've seen the color of the money."

I took the bait. "My lot? Know a lot of builders, do you?"

"Not sure. I don't usually ask for names, never mind professions." He grimaced when he registered what he'd said. "Sorry, that was—"

"It doesn't matter. How many of these nameless men did you invite back to your house? How many did you take out on your boat? How many presents did you take to their workplace?"

His gaze never left mine. "Zero."

I smiled. "Well, there you go, then, I'm special."

"You *are* special."

For a few glorious seconds, there was only the two of us. Age, location, and the fact it was freezing cold all ceased to matter. I was falling for him. Hell, that was a lie. I'd already fallen for him, and from the way he was looking at me, the feeling was mutual. My veins sang with all the possibilities of what the future could hold. It didn't matter what obstacles we'd need to overcome. Absentee parents. Different worlds. Disapproval from others. We could handle whatever came our way. I was sure of it.

I gave myself a mental shake before I became tempted to throw him down in the snow and take his virginity there and then. *What had we been talking about? Joking about builders, that was it.* I cleared my throat. "As for the deposit. Yes, it's required. How will I know you're good for it, if not?"

He came a step closer, his booted feet shuffling through the deep snow. "I'm definitely good for it."

"Talk is cheap."

"Oh, I can do actions as well."

Then his frozen lips were on mine, his arms wrapping around my neck as we set about generating enough shared heat that when we finally broke apart, I felt like I was on fire. Like someone had taken something dying and breathed life into it. I cupped his face with my gloved fingers, dropping a gentle kiss on his nose. "Every five minutes."

He held his arm up, peeling back his glove to reveal the expensive watch he always wore. "I'm going to set the alarm."

For the next couple of hours, we worked closely together, rolling and shaping snow to build a huge snowman. It would have been a lot faster save for the beeping of Tom's watch signaling the end of each five-minute period, the two of us reuniting to share a kiss and then giggling like a pair of schoolchildren caught doing something wrong. I frequently found myself pausing as well, taking the opportunity to watch him covertly just to revel in the sight of his happiness.

By my calculations, we were on about kiss fifteen when Tom suddenly grabbed hold of my arm, his voice urgent. "Look."

Despite the fact that I'd much rather have kept looking at him, I forced my gaze in the direction he was pointing. There was a pair of deer there: both male. They were nosing their way through the snow, searching for hidden foliage, seemingly unconcerned by our presence. Even as I thought that, one of them stepped closer, giving the snowman a cursory glance as if trying to work out why there was a huge man made of ice in the middle of their territory. Deciding it wasn't a threat, they continued their slow path past us. I'd known there were deer roaming free in Richmond Park; it was one of the things the park was renowned for. But I'd never actually seen them.

"Aren't they beautiful?"

I nodded, still watching them, my limbs starting to protest at the biting cold as I stayed still for far too long. It was time to get this snowman finished and drag Tom somewhere warm. *Like my bed.* Stepping back, I admired our collective work, the snowman looking pretty impressive if I said so myself. "What does it still need?"

Tom scanned it from head to toe. Or what would have been its toes had we gone into that level of detail. He crouched down, pulling a hat and scarf out of the bag he'd brought along. He grinned as he held the scarf in the air. "My dad's favorite Armani scarf."

"Maybe you shouldn't..."

But he was already wrapping it around the snowman's neck before adding the hat as well, which I assumed was his dad's too. He added a pair of sunglasses, which looked suspiciously like Ray-Bans. The snowman was going to be the best-dressed snowman in London. He stepped back, holding his arms aloft in a flourish. "Done."

I admired it for a moment. "Now what?"

Tom shrugged. "We take photos and then we go and sit in a lovely warm coffee house, and drink hot chocolate and eat cake for a few hours."

. . ⚓ . .

THE REST OF THE DAY passed in a blur. We had indeed sat in a coffee house for hours, sharing cake, talking, and laughing. Then, without either of us actually discussing it, we'd returned to Tom's house where he'd packed a bag with a couple of changes of clothing and other necessities such as his phone charger. When I'd insisted on him leaving a note for his parents in case they came back unexpectedly, he'd rolled his eyes but acquiesced. I didn't want the police knocking on my door because his parents weren't quite as blasé as he liked to make out. Respecting his privacy, I hadn't read the note, but couldn't help noticing how few words he'd written. I suspected it ran somewhere along the lines of, *I'm not dead. You don't need to look for me.*

And now there we were, sharing my bed, both of us stripped to our underwear. I glanced over to the nightstand, the dim lamp I'd left on illuminating the condoms and lube I'd left there earlier. We'd been building up to this point all day, but now that it had finally arrived, it seemed too momentous—the pressure of making it good almost suffocating me. What if he hated it? Where would that leave our fledgling relationship? I knew there was more to a gay relationship than anal. Of course there was. But Tom had been so keen to do it from the very first moment I'd met him that I had a feeling it would crush him if he didn't like it. It was possible that I was completely the wrong person to be trusted with something so special.

Tom rolled onto his back, his gaze roving over my face. "I can hear you worrying from here."

"I'm not. I'm just..." I couldn't give voice to my fears. I lay down, turning onto my side so that I faced him, my hand moving of its own volition to curl around his shoulder so I could feel the velvet softness of his skin beneath my fingertips. A sigh escaped from my lips.

He lifted his hand to cover mine, his thumb tracing the lumps and bumps of my knuckles. "We don't have to do anything you're not ready to do."

"No?" Even I could hear the disbelief in my voice. "You've been pretty clear about what you want since the moment I first met you."

A ghost of a smile pulled at his lips. "That was before."

"Before what?"

"It's stupid. Promise you won't laugh."

"Promise."

He exhaled slowly. "I had this ridiculous idea that if I could convince you to fuck me, it would bind you to me in some way and I'd get to keep you. I told you it was stupid. But now I feel like..."

I finished his sentence for him. "We're already bound together in some way."

"Yeah. Is that crazy?"

I shook my head, tamping down on the overwhelming rush of emotion at him basically admitting he felt the same way. "No, it's not crazy. Not at all. It should be, but... no."

Tom rolled onto his side so that we were facing each other, our heads a few inches apart. "So whatever happens is fine. Sex. No sex. Going to sleep. Just kissing. I'm just happy to be here with you."

I shuffled forward so that our noses were almost touching. "We're going to get sore lips if we keep kissing all the time."

"So worth it, though."

I couldn't argue with that statement, especially when my lips were already on his, Tom immediately opening up and our mouths moving greedily together, like there was no contact that would be quite enough to sate the passion in both of us. I had no idea how we'd gone from strangers in a bathroom stall to this in the space of only a few weeks. But it still wasn't enough. I wanted more. Whatever more was. I wanted his smiles. His conversation. His touch. His company. Everything. I wanted *him*. The good. The bad. And the ugly. However it had happened, he'd wormed his way under my skin and I had no intention of trying to reverse it.

I turned him in my arms, bringing us into the same position as the previous night, with his ass—underwear-clad this time rather than bare—tucked snugly against my crotch. I fastened my lips on his neck as he groaned and pushed back against me, his ass massaging my cock. My hands stole around him, following the hard planes of his chest, learning him by touch alone, from the jutting bones of his clavicle to the nipples that peaked beneath my fingertips as I touched them, before moving on to his flat abdomen. All the while I muttered words of nonsense in his ear: a mixture of endearments and compliments, telling him how gorgeous he was, how much I wanted him.

By the time I'd finished my exploration, my hands hovering at the waistband of his underwear, he was writhing against me, his skin hot against mine. He turned his head, stealing a kiss I was all too willing to give. I let my fingers dip below his waistband. Not far. Just far enough to feel the springy softness of his pubic hair against the tips of my fingers. As for my hips, they'd started a rhythm of their own volition. One that rocked my dick over and over again between Tom's ass cheeks, a clear simulation of penetration, saved from coming too close by the dual layer of fabric that still separated us.

Letting my fingers dip farther into his underwear, I was rewarded by a hard dick filling my hand. It fit perfectly against my palm as I began to stroke it, my hips grinding harder into his ass, the little moans escaping Tom's lips only adding fuel to the fire. I could have come like this, with nothing more than the friction of Tom's ass against me and him weak with desire in my arms. But it was as if him letting me off the hook on taking his virginity had enflamed me. Now that I felt like I didn't have to, it was all I could think about. With my free hand, I tugged at his waistband, Tom quickly reading my intent and cooperating as I divested him of his underwear, leaving him naked and aroused in my arms.

I maneuvered his body slightly, pushing him half onto his front, leaving enough room so I could continue to stroke his cock but at the same time giving me perfect access to his ass. I allowed myself the luxury of studying him for a few seconds, taking in everything from his goose-bumped skin to the flush of arousal on his chest. He was perfect. Completely perfect.

As if sensing my scrutiny, the dark sweep of his eyelashes lifted from his cheeks to reveal the gorgeous blue of his eyes. "Aiden." He managed to imbue that one word with so much need. So much longing, his desires reflecting my own perfectly. I knelt up, removing my own underwear before reaching across to the nightstand for the lube, adding a generous dollop to my fingers as well as a smear across the palm of the other hand that I'd been using to stroke his cock. Tom lay still in the position I'd placed him in, the relaxed curve of his muscular back demonstrating perfect trust. And hopefully I was going to reward that trust in spades.

I fitted my front against his back, my hand fisting Tom's cock again, his hips thrusting forward in search of greater friction. He stilled though as my other hand explored between his ass cheeks, painting delicate strokes of sensation over his taint before reaching his hole. I started with gentle touches, barely skimming the sensitive skin, driving him crazy with everything I wasn't doing, my name when it broke free from his lips sounding more like a curse. I kept up the friction on his cock, its solid length pulsing against my fingers.

Finally, I gave him what he was searching for, one finger pushing into the tight, clenching channel. I leaned over him, capturing his lips in order to distract him from what my hands were doing, to the point where he barely seemed to notice when one finger became two. I curled them, searching for his prostate, knowing I'd hit the right spot when he panted into my mouth. He quivered in my arms, tremors rolling through his taut frame. I slowed the movement of my hand over his cock, pulling my mouth from his to ask a question. "Are you close?"

Tom bit his lip, nodding jerkily at the same time. "So close."

I thrust my fingers deeper inside him, brushing his prostate again while I held his gaze. He was so much more relaxed than the previous time we'd tried this, his ass tipped up in perfect invitation. "Want me to make you come like this? Or do you want me to fuck you?" The final decision was his. I wasn't going to take it away from him, no matter how much I might yearn to put my cock in the same place I had my fingers.

There was no hesitation in his response. "I want to get fucked. I want you to be my first."

I didn't wait for any more clarification, releasing his cock from my grasp and withdrawing my fingers from his ass before reaching over to where I'd left the condoms. In no time at all, I had one on, my lubed cock resting between his ass cheeks while my hand returned to his cock. "This is probably still going to hurt, no matter how slow I take it."

"I know."

Stroking his cock harder in order to bring him back to the brink of orgasm, I lined myself up with his hole. Even a gentle pressure had him stiffening up. I kissed his neck, licking away the droplets of sweat that had collected there. "Relax. Just try and breathe deeply."

He did, and this time the tip of my cock breached him. I held still, giving him time to adjust before introducing another inch, my fingers digging into Tom's hip in an effort to keep both of our bodies under control. One more push and I was sheathed in him, his ass gripping me tightly as I exhaled. I fought against the urge to come right there and then, the emotional significance combining with the physical sensations in an overwhelming rush of pure pleasure. I breathed deeply, concentrating on remembering that this was for Tom. Not me.

Tom shifted slightly. "God! You feel so deep. So big. And it doesn't hurt." His voice was full of wonder. "I mean, it feels weird, but apart from that."

I chuckled against his neck. "Weird isn't exactly the feeling I was going for."

His hand closed over mine, encouraging me to renew the slick slide of my palm over his cock, the tip damp with pre-cum. "Maybe if you move."

"Shhh... patience." I wasn't sure whether the instruction was meant for him, myself, or both of us. If it had been meant for Tom, he clearly had no intention of listening, his ass gyrating against my crotch. I sought for control and lost the battle, pulling halfway out before thrusting back in. Tom made a noise, but it was more of surprise than discomfort, his body becoming soft and pliable as that first thrust turned into more until I was rutting against him, my balls already tight.

Then his body went rigid, heat spilling onto my palm as he came, his cock continuing to pulse long after the first spurt. Three more thrusts and I was joining him, my face buried in his hair as I almost choked with the intensity of the orgasm. It was only when I came back to Earth that I registered that although the prone body under mine felt fantastic, I was probably squashing him. I levered myself away, stroking his back when he flinched as I pulled my cock free from his ass.

I tied off the condom, dropping it in the bin and propping myself against the pillows before twisting my head around to stare at Tom's back. "Are you okay? Did I hurt you?"

With his head buried in the pillow, all I got was an incomprehensible noise which could have been any collection of words in the English language.

"What did you say?"

He rolled onto his back, a huge smile on his face. "I said, no, you didn't hurt me." He wriggled slightly, a twinge of discomfort crossing his face. "Although, I think my ass is going to be sore."

"Probably."

He glanced down at his torso where drops of cum still painted his skin. "Got a tissue?"

I passed one across, waiting until he'd cleaned up before taking it from him and dropping it in the bin to join the condom.

A satiated, sleepy gaze met mine. "How do you feel about cuddling?"

"Not normally a fan. But..." I lifted an arm, waiting until he'd shifted across the bed and snuggled close before I lowered it, wrapping him up in my embrace. "...for you I'll make an exception."

His eyes closed and I found myself unable to tear my gaze away as his breathing slowed. So this was what happiness felt like. Like I'd spent thirty-one years experiencing life rather than living it, before Tom had shaken it up in the very best way possible.

Chapter Twelve

It was the twenty-eighth of December. Tom and I had spent the last three days holed up together like a pair of newlyweds celebrating their honeymoon, barely able to keep their hands off each other. Thank God for the building site closing down over Christmas, providing me with those extra few days off work. Tomorrow though, I had to go back until the thirty-first—New Year's Day, of course, being a national holiday. I was used to spending New Year's Eve in the pub. This year, I couldn't see past spending it with Tom. He was the only person I wanted to see when the clock struck midnight to announce the start of a new year.

Tom was curled up on my sofa, looking for all the world as if he was reading a book. Only, he hadn't turned a page once in the last ten minutes. That and the far-away look in his eyes, revealed it for the pretense it was. I could only assume that my return to work was playing on his mind. "I only work nine till five you know? We can still see each other afterwards. And you can stay here if you don't want to go home. Although, you've probably got artsy things you need to be doing." He raised his head, staring at me blankly as if none of the words I'd said had processed at all, making me elaborate for his benefit. "I'm back at work tomorrow. I was just saying that we can still see each other. You should be glad I'm not a lawyer or an accountant, or whatever other professions work ridiculously long hours."

He nodded and I got the distinct impression that whatever was on his mind was something different. Walking over to the sofa, I sat down before pulling his bare feet onto my lap and massaging them. It seemed I did have a foot fetish when it came to him. Actually, it was more of a Tom fetish, where I adored every part of him. "We could go out for dinner tomorrow if you want? I never want to cook after working all day anyway."

"Dinner sounds good." He studied me from beneath lowered lids. "You're not worried about being seen with me?"

My lips curled into a smile. I knew where he was coming from but the question was still ridiculous. "You're right. If I get seen with someone so ridiculously hot, it might cause a huge wave of jealousy from anyone who sees us. Probably safer to stay in, just in case one of them is provoked into violence."

His lips quirked at the corners and I'd never been happier to see the beginnings of a smile. He rolled his eyes but it was full of affection. "You know what I meant."

I patted his foot. "No, I'm not bothered about being seen with you. Let people stare if they want to."

Tom placed his book down on the nearby table. "Shame I can't come to work with you. Guess I'd be useless on a building site, though."

"Oh, I don't know. You'd look cute wearing a hard hat, and you could, I don't know, pass me a hammer or something. Hold the cement tray. Make cups of tea. You could be my very sexy and glamorous assistant. The one that makes me want to sneak off into a dark corner and let you assist me in other ways far less suited to a working environment, and far more likely to get me fired."

This time, the smile was full-blown as he imagined the scene I'd set. I leaned forward, kissing the smile while it was still on his lips. "What will you do while I'm at work? Paint some more stunning pictures, maybe." I winked. "You could paint me if you want. Naked. Although, that should definitely stay facing the wall and it should probably stay here, rather than being anywhere near your parents."

The haunted look returned to his eyes, the smile melting away to nothing. My heart sank. *What had I said*? *Did he think I'd be offended if he didn't paint me?* I'd only meant it as a joke. The idea actually terrified me, given how good he'd shown himself to be at capturing people's characters and emotions on canvas. There were far worse things I could see immortalized in paint than my dick. Or perhaps it was nothing to do with the painting and more to do with the fractious relationship he had with his parents?

I decided the direct approach was best to try and get to the bottom of whatever was bothering him. "What's wrong? You can talk to me, you know. Maybe I can help. Are you worried about your parents coming back? Is that it? Are you concerned about what they might have to say about you seeing me?"

He shook his head. "They won't give a flying fuck. I mean, sure my mum will probably make some sort of cutting comment about me shopping for men in the over-thirties aisle. But that will be it. They don't care what I do, as long as it doesn't affect them."

I gave his feet a little shake. "So if it's not that, what is it? I know something's bothering you."

Blue eyes met mine, a strange emotion lurking in their depths that was difficult to identify. "I kind of did something and I don't know how to tell you."

My heart gave a jolt at the sincerity in his voice, my brain racing to try and work out what could possibly be so bad that he didn't want to admit to it. "What kind of something? Is it illegal?"

Tom gave a humorless laugh. "No, it's not illegal." He pulled his knees up and I let go of his feet as he shifted to sitting cross-legged so he could face me. "It's like you said a while ago, that I've always had everything handed to me on a plate. It's not like I didn't realize that myself. So a couple of months ago, I hatched a plan. I decided that I'd do something that had absolutely nothing to do with my parents. It was a crazy idea and I honestly thought it would come to nothing. But they liked my stuff. They really liked it."

He'd completely lost me. "Who liked it? Liked what? Can you back up a bit?"

He took a deep breath. "A couple of months ago, I applied for an art scholarship. They asked me to come for an interview, said they wanted to see more of my stuff... I'd had to send them photos as part of the application process, and they wanted a chat with me. I expected to get a 'thanks, but no thanks' letter in the post. But they called me in for another interview and then they offered me a full scholarship, said that I had immense talent and they didn't want to miss out on it."

I stared at him. Everything he'd said was great so I had no idea why he'd delivered it with such a sad expression. "That's fantastic! So you're going to do an art degree. I'm so happy for you. It's incredible news."

"Is it?" His eyes scrutinized my face as if he was searching for something. He visibly sagged, his shoulders slumping. "At the time, I wanted to make a clean break, get away from London, so I applied to the University of Dundee. Now..." He let the unfinished sentence hang there.

I finally understood, picturing the scenario he was describing. Me in London, him, hundreds of miles away in Scotland, a whole chasm of distance between us. Despite the pounding of my heart as reality set in, I sought to remain calm and keep things in perspective. "Okay. Well, it's not until next year, right? So... anything could happen between now and then."

"They want me to start in January. January the tenth."

"January?" I echoed the word, feeling like someone had driven a knife into my heart. "As in a couple of weeks from now?" I did my utmost to keep the emotion I was feeling from showing on my face, but I had a sneaking suspicion, given the way he was looking at me, that I was doing a pretty piss-poor job. The last few days had been perfect and now I was facing the prospect of that being it. That my newfound happiness was about to be ripped away from me by something so innocuous as an art scholarship.

His gaze slid away from mine. "I should have told you before. I'm sorry."

"Before what?" My voice sounded like it belonged to someone else, someone giving a really good impression of speaking in a calm and measured way, despite their insides tumbling around like a washing machine in full flow.

"Before we... before you..." Tom ducked his head, a flush appearing on his sharp cheekbones. I never quite understood how he could go from being so sexually confident one minute to appearing almost shy the next. But it was all part and parcel of what I liked about him. He peeped at me from beneath his lashes. "You know, the losing-the-virginity thing. You're going to think I deliberately withheld information to trick you into doing it."

"I don't feel tricked." I didn't. Once the hurdle of the dreaded virginity label had been discarded, we'd repeated it the next night. Only this time much longer and slower, Tom looking up at me, his ankles draped over my shoulders as I fucked him to orgasm while memorizing the expression of utter bliss he wore. No matter what happened in the future, they were memories I'd always treasure. Along with the snowman building, and the lazy afternoon spent drinking hot chocolate. Hell, even falling in a freezing cold river had become tinged with a rose-tinted-glasses sentimentality.

Tom brought his knees up, wrapping his arms around them and resting his chin on the top. "Anyway, I've been thinking and I'm not going to go. I'm going to call them and say thanks for the offer but I've changed my mind."

I stared at him. "Why?"

He sighed. "Numerous reasons. I mean, is it fair that I'm accepting a scholarship when I could have asked my parents for the money? And they would have given it to me. Hugs. Kisses. Love. No way." His mouth twisted. "But money's easy. What if I'm taking that scholarship away from someone else? Someone who can't afford to study without it?"

I shook my head in denial of the point he was making. "You earned it. And the whole point is that you wanted to do something independent of your parents. Which includes not asking them for the money. Right?"

He nodded, his eyes intent on my face. "There's other reasons, though."

"Such as?"

But we both knew.

His head dropped forward onto his knees, his voice muffled and indistinct. "I hadn't met you then. I didn't have anything to stay in London for. We've just started building something." He raised his head, a look of anguish on his face. "I already love you, Aiden. I know it sounds crazy because we've only known each other a few weeks and you spent half of that time pushing me away because you thought I was too young for you. But it's true. And I'm old enough to know my own mind before you throw that one at me."

My heart settled into an even crazier rhythm until it felt as if it would force itself right out of my chest. "It's not crazy." I'd already known that what we'd shared in the past few days was love. We'd slotted together too easily for it to be anything else. Both of us found it much easier than it should have been to go from spending the majority of the time on our own to being happy in someone else's company 24/7. The feelings were too intense. The emotions too colorful. The silences too meaningful. We just hadn't addressed it. Until now. "I love you too."

"You do?" He shuffled forward so that he was almost in my lap, a tremulous smile lighting up his whole face. "So you understand why I can't go, then? I can ask my parents for the money and apply to somewhere in London next year. It doesn't mean I can't do an art degree. Just not yet, and not where I was planning to go. You agree, right?"

My gaze lingered on his face as I considered it. It would be so easy to say yes. If I did, Tom's life would continue in the same vein as it had previously. The only difference would be that he'd have me in it. I could ask him to move in, but he'd still be alone while I was at work. Maybe it would change once he secured a place at a local university. Or perhaps the fact that he had a boyfriend waiting at home for him would hold him back.

He already found it difficult to make meaningful connections with people—to make genuine friends. I didn't want to be the reason it would be even more difficult. He'd end up turning down the opportunity for social connections he needed so he could be with me. Of course he'd say it was fine. That it was his choice. But the damage would already be done. If he went to Dundee, he'd have a real chance to break free. To have a fresh start in a place where no one would have the faintest clue that he came from money. He'd just be the beautiful boy with the gorgeous blue eyes and the amazing art talent. The one people would want to get to know solely for who he was. For one crazy moment, I considered offering to go with him. But my sister was here. My niece was here. Not to mention my house and my job. It just wasn't feasible.

"Aiden?"

There was a well-known saying, "*if you love someone, set them free.*" I'd never understood it before. But right now, with my heart clamoring in my chest, and a feeling of nausea blooming like I was two seconds away from being sick, I understood it perfectly. Tom had made plans. Plans to change his life for the better. I could love him enough to encourage those plans for his own good or I could be the obstacle that held him back. "You have to go." Those four words were the hardest words I'd ever forced myself to say.

He reared back, an expression of absolute hurt blossoming on his face. I may as well have slapped him. "Why would you say that? Don't you want me? That doesn't make sense. You just said you love me. I heard you say it." He shook his head. "Why would you tell me that and then less than five minutes later tell me to go? Is it the age thing again? Because, if so..."

I shushed him, wiping away the tear that slowly rolled down his cheek and ignoring my breaking heart. "Listen to me, Tom. You're going to go to Dundee. You're going to make friends. You're going to study hard and play hard as well. You're going to create a whole new life for yourself. One that you deserve."

"*You* won't be there."

I wiped away more tears as they fell until their frequency was such that I was fighting a losing battle and had to give up. "Three years isn't such a long time. Who knows, maybe you'll want to come back to London then, and I'll still be here waiting." I forced a smile, even though it felt like I was the instigator of my own downfall. "Even more of an old man than I am now."

Tom's headshake was emphatic. "You say that now, but you'll change your mind. You'll find someone else."

I pulled him into my arms, letting his tears soak into my shoulder. It was hard not to wonder whether I'd just made the biggest mistake of my life. But then, I wasn't doing it for myself—I was doing it for him. If it meant he could be happy in the long-term, then it was worth upsetting him in the short-term. Then, whatever the outcome for the two of us might be, it would still be worth it.

Chapter Thirteen

January 7th

"At least the snow's cleared."

Tom nodded at my poor attempt to make conversation. "It's still cold though."

I stamped my feet on the train platform, trying to force some feeling back into my toes. Everything in the last week and a half had been leading up to this point. The inevitable moment where I'd have to smile and wave as Tom walked out of my life. I scanned the nearly empty platform; there were only a few people waiting for the same train. "I thought your parents might show up to say goodbye."

The noise out of Tom's mouth was half bitter laugh, half huff of surprise that I'd even suggest it. "They already said their goodbyes. Sort of."

"Yeah?"

Tom shifted his suitcase slightly to the left with his foot. "My mum made some sort of insinuation about me whoring my way around Scotland, and my dad pointed out that I should take an umbrella because it rains a lot up there." He paused. "Actually, that's quite considerate for him." He shrugged. "But yeah, that was about it. It doesn't matter. I didn't expect anything more from them."

I glanced up to the departure board. The train was due in eight minutes. Eight minutes—that's what my life had come down to. Eight minutes in which to say everything I desperately needed to say. Except my mind had gone blank, so we stood in silence. I wanted to reach out and hold his hand, but it seemed hypocritical when I was there to see him off. Instead, I had to settle for standing so close our shoulders touched. I searched around for something to break the silence. "And you've got a place to stay there, haven't you?"

He nodded. "I've got a room in the residence halls. It'll be a bit weird at first because everyone else will have been there since September, but hopefully it'll be okay."

"Maybe I should have come with you. Made sure you were settled in."

Tom shook his head before turning to face me. "No. It would have just made it more difficult."

We both glanced at the departure board at the same time. *Six minutes.*

He turned his head slightly to the side and I caught the sparkle of unshed tears. "Please don't cry."

Tom dashed at his eyes with the back of his gloved hand. "I'm trying really hard not to." He took a deep, calming breath. "We both need to remember that no one died. And I'm going to Scotland, not outer Mongolia. It's a few hours away, not the other side of the world."

It was a valid point, but it didn't make the impending separation hurt any less. "I know, right."

Five minutes.

He crossed his arms. "What will you do tonight?"

Miss you. Wonder what the hell I was thinking to send you away. Probably sniff the pillow where your head's lain for the last couple of weeks like a lovelorn idiot. Cry. I shrugged. "Probably go to the pub down the road."

Tom's smile was wistful. "I have fond memories of that pub."

"So do I."

Four minutes.

I stamped my feet again. "I wonder what you'll end up doing tonight."

"I expect I'll be too busy unpacking and trying to work out where everything is to do anything."

"Probably. Just don't get lost."

Tom pulled his iPhone out of his pocket, waving it in the air between us. "Is that even possible in this day and age? I just follow the blue dot and voila."

Three minutes.

And then I heard the worst sound in the world, the noise of an approaching train. It was early. Of course it was. Any other day it would have been delayed and I would have had longer. Tom stepped in front of me, his hands reaching up to grasp the lapels of my coat to pull me closer. "Kiss me."

I pulled my gloves off, needing to feel skin, and cupped his face. I put everything I had into that kiss. My longing. My desire. My regret. My gratitude. My love. Tom met it with equal intensity, clinging to me like he never wanted to let go. The kiss that had started out as hard and crushing finally petered into soft and lingering. A perfect reflection of our entire relationship.

Someone pushing past us proved the catalyst for breaking us apart, the train now stationary. Tom stepped away and picked up his suitcase. "I have to go."

I nodded, my throat so thick I wasn't sure I'd be able to produce words even if I tried.

He took a couple of steps backward in the direction of the train, his face tight and another stray tear inching its way down his cheek. "I'll call you. Probably all the time. You'll get sick of hearing from me. And I'll be home for holidays. We'll see each other then."

I managed another nod.

"I love you, Aiden."

I forced my mouth to open, grateful when sound did come out, even though it sounded wispy and thin and nothing like my normal voice. "I love you too."

And then, with one last lingering glance, he turned his back and boarded the train. There was a seat free close to where he'd boarded, meaning I got to study his face for a few precious seconds longer, committing his features to memory. The train started pulling away and I lifted my hand and waved, Tom returning the gesture. And then I couldn't see him anymore.

No minutes.

I didn't give in to my own tears until the train was no longer in sight. The last thing Tom had needed to see was that I was just as cut up as he was. He might have done something stupid like refuse to leave and I would have caved. I know I would have. The selfish streak would have taken over. It had been hard enough to hold firm over the last few days when everything inside me had been screaming that I shouldn't let him go.

I walked slowly to the exit, managing to get myself under control by the time I stepped out onto the street. A familiar ear-piercing whistle rent the air and I turned to find JT leaning nonchalantly against the railing. He raised a hand and waved as I walked over to him. "What are you doing here?"

He grinned. "Took the afternoon off, didn't I, to come and look after your sorry ass. We're going to the pub."

I shook my head, confused. "Why?"

He scoffed at me. "Why? Because you might think I'm just a blind, insensitive oaf but I am actually aware that you've just put your boyfriend, who you happen to be head over heels in love with, on a train and you don't know when you'll see him again."

I stared at him. "Jules asked you to come, didn't she?"

He placed a hand on his chest in mock hurt before breaking into a laugh. "Yeah, she did actually. Gave me strict instructions to feed you, get you drunk, let you cry on my shoulder without complaining, and to bring you back to ours if you don't want to be on your own tonight."

I swallowed, touched by her concern. "She's one hell of a woman, your wife."

JT slapped me on the back, before tugging me over in the direction of the high street. "And don't I know it. Probably because she tells me every day what a lucky man I am."

Chapter Fourteen

January 12th

It was good to hear Tom's voice on the other end of the line. "So have you settled in?"

"Just about. Charlie, the guy in the room next to me, has been really friendly. He's kind of taken me under his wing and keeps inviting me out with his friends. None of whom seem to be coke-snorting weirdos, so that's always a bonus."

"And is Charlie...?" *Fuck!* I stopped myself from asking the question just in time. I floundered for a moment, all other words in the English language suddenly deserting me.

Tom gave a little snort. "Were you about to ask me if he was gay? Are you insinuating that he's only befriended me because he's after my body?"

"No. Of course not."

"He's straight, Aiden. Or at least that's what his girlfriend seems to think. I think the only one in the group who's gay is Cav. Well, and me as well now, I guess, assuming they don't get bored of me. I start my course tomorrow so I'll get to meet some more people then. How have you been doing?"

I fixed my gaze on the wall, running a number of possible responses through my head. *Not great. I've been wishing I never opened my big mouth and convinced you to go. Everything seems so much greyer without you here.* "I've been doing fine. You know, busy with work and stuff."

"Ah, the busy world of building."

There was a squeaking sound like he'd opened a drawer and I wondered what he was up to. Whether he was alone or there was someone else there with him. "Well, things don't build themselves."

"They certainly don't."

There was a long pause. "I miss you, Aiden."

"I miss you too."

January 15th

"Hello."

Tom's voice sounded harried when he finally answered and I wondered whether I'd chosen a bad time. "Hi, it's me. I just thought I'd call. See how the start of your course went."

"Aiden." There was genuine warmth in Tom's voice, which did a lot to put my mind at ease, given how he'd answered the call. He must not have checked the caller ID before picking up. "Yeah, it's going well. I've learnt a lot already and most of my fellow students seem like a really cool bunch. There were a couple of others who joined in January as well, so we've kind of banded together. What about you?"

"Same old."

"Nothing exciting happening in the building world?"

I laughed. "Not that I've noticed."

There was a sudden onslaught of voices in the background on Tom's end. "Hang on. One minute, Aiden."

I waited as some sort of conversation happened that was too faint for me to hear. Finally, Tom came back on the line. "Sorry about that. Cav wanted to invite me to a party at his friend's house. But I told him I was talking to you."

"Cav?"

"Yeah, Charlie's friend. The one I told you about before."

The gay one. I remembered. "You should go. You don't want to be missing out on stuff. We can talk any time."

"Are you sure?"

The fact that he hadn't tried to argue spoke volumes about him wanting to go. I wondered what the attraction was. The party? Or the man that had offered the invite? I immediately felt guilty. Less than two weeks ago, Tom had been telling me he loved me. Even the ficklest person wouldn't move on that quickly, and as far as I was concerned, he was far from fickle. "Yes, of course. Have a good time."

There was the sound of a kiss being blown and a quick goodbye before the line went dead. It was good that Tom was getting a social life. After all, wasn't it exactly what I'd wanted for him? I needed to back off for a while and let him get settled without me hounding him.

February 5th

My phone buzzed in my pocket. I pulled it out to see Tom's name on the screen. I quickly pressed the button to answer the call and held it up to my ear. "Tom?"

Someone dropped a glass and what seemed like the entire pub erupted into the timely tradition of cheering broken glass, successfully drowning out whatever Tom had just said. I shouted into the phone as I stood. "Hang on. I'm going to go somewhere quieter." I shouldered my way through the crowd of people—tonight was quiz night—until I stepped out onto the street, which contained a few smokers but was a hell of a lot quieter than the interior of the pub had been. I swapped my phone to the other ear. "That's better. Are you still there?"

"Yeah, I'm still here. Where are you? Sounds like a party or something."

"Just at the pub. It's a bit rowdier than it is usually. It's quiz night. More JT's scene than mine, but I lost a bet with him over something stupid so here I am." The long silence clued me in to the fact that something was up. "Did you just call to find out what I was doing tonight?" The sigh that escaped from Tom's mouth echoed down the phone line as I waited for his response.

"Don't be mad at me."

My heart started to pound in anticipation of whatever piece of news he was finding it difficult to say. *Was this where he was going to tell me he'd met someone else?* "What is it?"

"I'm not coming back to London at Easter."

I let out a slow breath. It wasn't great news, but it was still better than the alternative. "Why not?"

"I just... I don't think it would be a good idea. Not yet. Maybe during the summer. I've only been here two minutes. I feel like I've only just got settled."

It took a great deal of effort to manage to form my mouth around the word, "okay."

"Is it?"

Slumping back against the wall, I reminded myself that this was what I'd wanted. For him to start living his life. It should be good news that he wouldn't be returning to his old life any time soon, but it still felt like someone had punched me in the stomach. I remembered his tearful assurance at the train station when we'd said goodbye that he would be home for the holidays. Yet in a matter of weeks, he'd already changed his mind. It didn't bode well for the future. For us. *Was there even an us anymore? Or was he trying to tell me something else with this conversation?* I cleared my throat. "Yeah, of course. You do what you need to do. I want to see you, but I understand if you don't think that feels right at the moment."

"I want to see you too, but—"

"You don't need to explain."

There was an awkward silence where neither of us seemed to know what to say. It dragged on for far too long before I broke it. "I better go. The quiz is about to start."

"Sure. I'll speak to you soon, Aiden."

"Yeah, soon."

I hung up, leaned back against the wall, and closed my eyes, staying there until JT came out to find me.

February 14th

Aiden: *Just wanted to wish you Happy Valentine's Day. I tried calling but you're probably busy. X*

February 15th

Tom: *Sorry. There's been a lot going on. Happy belated Valentine's Day to you too. X*

March 3rd

Tom: *Just realized how long it's been since we last spoke. I've had exams. Yes, even art students have exams. How did your sister's birthday go?*

Aiden: *It went fine. Have you got time for a chat and I'll tell you all about it?*

Tom: *Damn. Not right now. Sorry. I've got to get a painting finished by tomorrow. I'll call soon though.*

April 5th

I sat bolt upright in bed, trying to work out what could have woken me. A sideways glance at the clock revealed it to be three in the morning. It also brought my vibrating phone on the nightstand into my peripheral vision. It must have been that which had woken me. I picked it up cautiously—unexpected phone calls in the middle of the night were never good news. I don't know whose name I'd expected to see—my sister's maybe, but it certainly wasn't Tom's, given that communication between the two of us had been so sparse lately. Snatching the phone up, I managed to answer it before it went to voicemail, all sorts of scenarios flitting through my brain at rapid speed. *Was he hurt? Did he need help?* "Tom? Are you okay? What's wrong?"

"Nothing's wrong. I just needed to talk to you."

I relaxed back against the pillows as his voice came out slurred. There was no panic. He was just drunk. Tom probably hadn't even realized what time it was. "About what?"

"Us."

The word hit me like a twelve-ton truck and I already knew what was coming. He'd probably gotten drunk so he could pluck up the courage to have this conversation. Actually, we probably didn't even need to have it. Communication dwindling to virtually nothing had said all there was to say. The inevitable outcome had been staring me in the face for longer than I cared to admit. I'd just clung on to a tiny thread of hope that perhaps I was wrong, that perhaps he'd just been really busy. I didn't know what to say. I made some sort of noise in my throat which could have meant anything.

"We need to live our own lives, Aiden."

And there it was. A few simple words that stole all the oxygen from my lungs. The sad thing was that he was right. "I know."

"It's not healthy, the two of us in limbo like this. We're too far apart to make it work. And I'm just not in the right headspace to come home yet. I'm scared that if I do, I won't want to come back, which probably sounds crazy. But it's the truth. I've been agonizing over this. I really have. But it's the best thing for both of us. It's not fair of me to expect you to wait.

"I know that too. I just hoped..." I couldn't finish the sentence, because deep down I'd known all along that it would come to this. I'd convinced myself that I'd loved him enough to set him free, except really, I hadn't at all, I'd just put him on a long leash. "I won't call you anymore."

Tom made a noise that lay somewhere between a sigh and a sob. His voice suddenly grew louder as if he'd pulled the phone closer to his mouth. "But I need you to know this, Aiden. It doesn't mean I don't love you. Just that it's not our time yet. After I finish this degree, I'm coming for you and you better not have fallen in love with anyone else. You can date them. You can fuck them. You just can't..." His voice broke mid-sentence. "I'll fight for you if I have to."

I shook my head even though I knew he couldn't see it. "That's the drink talking."

"No, it's not. It's the drink making me brave enough to say it. Just because I'm letting you go doesn't mean you're not mine. We're meant to be together one day. Do you know how I know that?"

"How?"

"Cav kissed me." The words carried less of a blow than I expected. Maybe because it was another thing that had been obvious. Tom and I might not have spoken that much in the last few weeks but whenever we did the other man's name had always come up. They'd been spending more and more time together. I was thankful that Tom didn't wait for any response before continuing, because I didn't have a fucking clue what I was supposed to say to that. *Congratulations? I'm happy for you both?* "It was nice. But it was nothing like kissing you. You and I made fireworks. Cav barely made a... I can't even think of a comparison that fits. So when the time's right, I'm coming back for those fireworks. Is that selfish?"

I didn't know whether to laugh or cry. All I could do was be honest. "I'll be waiting."

Tom's voice dropped to a soft whisper, all traces of drunkenness seemingly gone. "I hope you are."

For a moment, neither of us spoke, as if we needed that extra few seconds of listening to the other one breathe.

"Bye, Aiden."

I bit my lip, hoping the pain would be enough to stave off my breakdown long enough for the call to have ended. "Bye, Tom."

Then there was the click of the phone disconnecting and nothing to stop me from giving in to the feeling of utter devastation. Even though I knew it was the right thing for both of us, it didn't stop it from hurting. I had a feeling nothing and no one would ever ease that pain apart from Tom himself.

Chapter Fifteen

*C*hristmas Day. Three years later.

Anabelle sighed, holding up the angel between her thumb and fore-finger. "Don't you think it's about time you got rid of this?"

I snatched it out of her hands, just in case she was tempted to put her plan into action without my say-so. "No! I don't."

She gave an even longer sigh. "I'm worried you're going to end up like the male version of Miss Havisham, only minus the wedding dress, still sitting here in ten years waiting for something that's not going to happen. He finished his degree five months ago, Aiden. If he was going to turn up out of the blue to... win your hand back, don't you think he'd have done it by now?"

"I don't know." My subconscious immediately fought against how much sense I knew her words made. But I wasn't ready to extinguish that tiny ember of hope that lived on somewhere deep in my chest. Not yet. Maybe I never would be. Anabelle could be right. I'd grow old and die, still clutching on to the exquisite angel that had been made especially for me decades ago.

I'd gotten on with my life just as I'd said I would. A promotion to foreman had brought less hours and more financial security. My niece—who was sitting on the floor playing with dolls—was spoilt rotten by her doting uncle. And I'd dated. Nothing serious that had lasted any longer than a couple of months, but it wasn't like I'd sat in an attic covered in cobwebs like my sister was making out.

I had to admit, though, it was hard to recall a single day when I hadn't thought of Tom at least once. He was always there in the back of my mind, random things bringing him to the forefront. The grey scarf a woman wore re-minding me of the one he'd wrapped around the snowman's neck. The smell of hot chocolate bringing to mind the one we'd shared. A song that had been played at Winter Wonderland bringing a fond smile to my lips with memories of the time we'd spent there. And every damn flake of snow that had fallen over the last three years prompted a vivid recall of blue eyes, cold cheeks, and lips meeting mine for the very first time.

Walking over to the table, I placed the angel carefully back at its center. I didn't put it on the tree anymore. I wasn't sure why. Worried about it getting damaged maybe? Or perhaps I just needed it closer. A physical reminder that the time spent with Tom hadn't been a figment of my imagination.

Annabelle crouched down, packing Grace's dolls away into a bag before helping her daughter into her coat. "Say thank you to Uncle Aiden for the presents and for making Christmas dinner."

Grace skipped toward me, her blonde plaits bouncing up and down with the motion. "Thank you, Uncle Aiden." I picked her up and swung her round until she giggled. Then I planted a noisy kiss on her cheek before lowering her back to the ground. "You're welcome, pumpkin. Look after your mum on the way home. Hold her hand really tightly."

The three-year-old nodded somberly as only three-year-olds could. Anabelle pulled on her own coat before crossing the room to brush a kiss across my cheekbone. "You never should have let him go. You know that, right? You should have hung on to him with all your might. Self-sacrifice is so overrated."

It wasn't the first time we'd had this conversation and I doubted it would be the last. "I wanted him to be happy."

She pulled a face. "Even if it means you're not? It would have been easier if he'd died. At least then you'd have been able to grieve and move on. But this... this isn't fair, what he's done to you. He made you fall for him and then he upped and left. And if that wasn't bad enough, he made you believe he was coming back once he'd finished his degree." She held her arms aloft. "Where is he?"

I shook my head. I hated it when she got on her high horse about Tom. She'd never met him, so I couldn't blame her to a certain extent. And I knew it was her way of being protective but it made things worse, rubbed salt into what was already a weeping sore. I walked her to the door, seeing the two of them out and waiting until Grace had stopped twisting around to wave before letting myself back in. Then there was nothing but silence to contend with. Silence and memories made worse by my sister's well-meaning but ill-timed advice.

I'd been dozing for a couple of hours when the knock at the door sounded. I struggled to my feet, rubbing my eyes as I stumbled toward it. When I wrenched it open, though, there was no one there. I was about to damn the neighborhood's kids to hell for ruining my sleep when my eyes fell on the large, flat parcel wrapped in bright Christmas paper leaning against the door. *What the hell!* Sighing, I picked it up, turning it over and over in my hands. There was no tag, which meant that although it had obviously been left at the wrong house, I had no way of working out where it was supposed to be.

Even if I tried taking it around to my neighbors' houses, it was unlikely—unless one of them had been expecting a hit-and-run Christmas present delivery—that they'd know it was for them either. With no other clues to go on, I tugged at the corner of the paper. Perhaps knowing the contents would narrow it down. The paper came away easily to reveal the corner of a canvas. A bolt of memories hit me square in the chest and I had to take a calming breath. *For fuck's sake.* I guess I needed to add paintings to my ever-growing list of triggers.

I uncovered more, until the entire front of the painting had been revealed. It was a beautiful painting, each detail perfectly rendered, which meant I had no problems recognizing the familiar scene it depicted. A snowy river. Two figures on a boat. The brushstrokes capturing the larger figure perfectly as he teetered on the edge of the boat, seconds away from plunging backward into the freezing water.

My heart skipped. This wasn't just memories. There was only one person who could have painted this. The knowledge left me momentarily dizzy. *Had Tom been here? Or had he gotten someone else to drop it off for him? Why? What was he trying to tell me by leaving a reminder of our time together?*

"Merry Christmas, old man. Did I wake you?"

For a moment, I froze. It was safer to keep staring at the painting. Because, what if I turned and there was nobody there? What if I'd never woken up and this was just a dream conjured up by the recent conversation with my sister. Only, I could feel the cold from the concrete beneath my bare feet. I could feel the bite of the icy wind through the thin T-shirt I wore. That wasn't possible in a dream. Which meant this was real. That he was really there.

I turned slowly in the direction the achingly familiar voice had come from. And there he was. Tom. In the flesh. His hands pushed into the pockets of a long, black coat, a navy-blue scarf wrapped around his throat. No hat, though. He looked the same, but yet subtly different at the same time. His face that little bit fuller with maturity. His shoulders that little bit broader, discernible even beneath the thick coat. But his eyes were the same, that gorgeous blue color I remembered so well. My eyes devoured him, almost unable to believe he was actually standing there right in front of me.

He shifted uncomfortably under my scrutiny, a muscle twitching in his cheek. "Say something, Aiden, please."

"Like what?" My voice sounded as if I'd spent the last couple of hours gargling with razor blades.

A smile wavered on his lips before disappearing. "Like, hello. Or where have you been, you bastard?"

I shook my head, still trying to clear the feeling that reality had warped in some way.

"Should I go?"

My gaze flicked from Tom to the painting and then back again, trying to fit all of the pieces together. "No."

He exhaled loudly, relief flashing across his face. "Can I come in, then?"

"You painted this?" As questions went, it had to be one of the dumbest. How many other artists did I know who happened to be there that day?

He came to stand next to me, our shoulders touching. I closed my eyes for a few seconds at the pang of longing that hit me at his proximity. "Yeah, I did. A couple of years ago, actually. But I wanted to give it to you, face to face. Or I did until I got here and then I chickened out. I suddenly had this crazy fear that you might not live here any longer so I knocked and hid like a naughty schoolboy."

I stated the obvious. "I still live here."

"Alone?"

The simple question was loaded with so much subtext, but all I could do was state the truth. "Yes."

"Can I come in?"

It was the second time Tom had asked that same question. I nodded, moving aside to allow him access and following him inside with the painting in my hand. I leaned it against the wall of my living room and watched Tom as he turned around in a slow circle with a huge smile on his face. "Oh my God! It looks the same." His eyes caught sight of something on the table, his smile growing wider as he crossed the room in a few strides, sweeping the angel off the table and into his hand. He held it up to the light. "You kept it."

I shrugged. I still felt as if I were whirling around in some sort of parallel universe. One question kept pushing itself to the forefront of my mind. *Why are you here?* I just couldn't bring myself to ask it. What if I didn't get the answer I wanted? What if the words out of Tom's mouth were nothing to do with coming back for me, and everything to do with closure?

Tom still moved around the room, examining each little thing he came across as if it was something precious. He ran a hand across the back of the sofa. The same sofa we'd given each other blow jobs on. The same sofa where he'd napped when he'd turned up drunk exactly three years ago to the very day. The same sofa where he'd been so miserable when he'd admitted applying for the scholarship.

I continued to scrutinize him, trying to discern an answer to the question still hammering at my brain from his actions and body language. There was a lightness about him that never used to be there. The Tom I'd known had always seemed like he carried the weight of the world on his shoulders. He looked happy, and it looked good on him. He disappeared into the kitchen while I hung back in the living room. Thankfully, he seemed to draw the line at checking out the bedroom.

Finally, he stepped back into the living room, his eyes intent on my face. "You don't seem very happy to see me?"

Happy? I didn't know what I was. Bruised, maybe. Feeling like a wound that had been stitched and bandaged and then had faded to a scar had suddenly opened up again. I took a deep breath. "I don't know why you're here. Why now?"

Tom tilted his head to the side as if considering my words carefully. "You're angry at me for not coming sooner. I thought you might be."

"No, I'm not angry, I'm..." I shook my head in frustration. "How can I be angry when I didn't think you'd come at all? And then you just turn up."

Realizing he was still wearing his coat, Tom slipped it off, laying it over the back of the sofa. He did the same with his scarf before fastening his gaze back on me, an expression of hurt on his face. "You doubted me? I told you I was going to come back for you."

The noise that came out of my mouth was half laugh, half sigh. "You were drunk, and in case you've forgotten, that was nearly three years ago. We haven't spoken, texted, or anything since."

Tom came a step closer. "But I always meant it. You were never far from my thoughts. I meant every single word I said. So the question is, did you?"

"Did I what?"

He swallowed nervously, his eyes wide and unblinking, his body far too still. "Fall in love with anyone else?"

It struck me how easy it would be to say yes. He'd pick up his coat and leave and I'd probably never see him again. "I've dated."

He nodded, taking another step closer. "And what happened?"

"No fireworks. Barely even a flame. What about you?"

His lips twitched as if he was suppressing a smile. "Same. It felt like going through the motions."

The question had to be asked, the same one I hadn't thanked my sister for voicing a few hours ago. "Your degree finished in July. That was five months ago."

He grimaced. "I know. A friend of mine needed help so I stayed in Dundee. He was having a lot of family problems. I didn't feel like I could leave him until things were more stable. Which took until the beginning of December. And then..." He hesitated. "...I don't know, it sounds stupid but I wanted to wait for Christmas." Tom smiled wryly. "To me, we've always been Christmas. That little slice of perfection surrounded by snow, lights, and god-awful music."

There was no stopping the smile from blossoming on my face. Not when I knew exactly what he meant. He closed the remaining space between us, his hands coming up tentatively to rest on my chest as his head tipped back to maintain eye contact. "You can send me away if you want, but I need you to know first that I never stopped loving you. You gave me the biggest sacrifice that anyone could ever give me. You pushed me away so that I had the time and the space to learn how to be happy. And I did. I made friends. I developed a skill. I learned to love myself. But there was always a piece missing. And that piece was you."

I don't know who made the first move. Me? Him? Or maybe it was both of us. All I knew was that one minute we were staring into each other's eyes and the next we were kissing. Not a gentle "let's get reacquainted" kiss, but a passionate, "oh my God, I've missed you so much" kiss. And the spark was still there. That mixture of passion and sweetness that I'd only ever been able to find with one man. *This* man. I crushed him to me, lifting his thighs and wrapping them around my waist before backing him against the wall.

The kiss said everything we hadn't been able to put into words. We still loved each other. We still needed each other. Years might have gone by and we might both have been with other people, but there'd always, metaphorically, been three people in both of our beds. We kissed like we couldn't get enough of each other, our hands stroking over skin while tongues and lips teased and tasted. The two of us kissed until we finally reached a point where we were willing to relinquish the other one's mouth.

Tom rested his forehead against mine. "You understand, right? Why I had to go and live my own life. If I'd come back before, I'd never have left again. It was so hard leaving you the first time. I couldn't go through that again, even for holidays."

I let his legs slide to the floor, leaving him propped up against the wall. "Of course I understood. You needed to grow up."

He chuckled. "It always comes back to age, doesn't it? I'll have you know that I'm twenty-one."

I raised an eyebrow. "Wow! Positively ancient. You might be a bit too old for me now." Realizing I was talking as if everything was a foregone conclusion, I forced myself to slow down. "I mean, assuming that we're on the same page here."

He traced my bottom lip with his thumb, the look in his eyes nothing short of adoration. "I'm moving back to London. Well, I kind of already have. I refused to go back to the house in Richmond, though, so I've been staying at a cheap hotel instead. I want you. But I'm not stupid. I realize I'm just waltzing back into your life as if the last three years never happened. So, I'm willing to take it as slow as you need. I'll wine you. Dine you. Bring you flowers. Serenade you, if you want."

"Can you sing?"

He threw his head back and laughed. "Not really."

"So that last one was more of a threat?"

"Probably."

I stared at him, still finding it difficult to believe that this was happening. "And the flowers. Are they going to be delivered to the building site?"

He grinned. "Will that get you into trouble with your boss?"

"I am the boss."

Tom whistled through his teeth. "Oh, like that is it." He went suddenly quiet. "I know I'm contradicting what I said about taking it slow, but I would really love it if you took me to bed."

Both my heart and my dick twitched, the two organs in complete agreement that they would love it too. "Are you sure?"

He grasped my hand, dragging it down his body until my fingers curled around the hard dick pushing at the fabric. "Definitely sure. You were my first, and without sounding too cheesy, I want you to be my last."

Any doubt I'd been holding on to scattered into dust at the bold announcement. It would work this time. It had to. Because one thing was for sure, I might have let him go once, but that wasn't going to happen again. I picked him up, carrying him into the bedroom and dropping him gently onto the bed, the love I felt for him no doubt plastered across my face as I stared down at him. I didn't care since it was reflected straight back at me.

Three years. It had been a long time. But who the fuck cared? Tom was back and he was mine. That's all that mattered.

Epilogue

I lifted my arm in invitation and Tom snuggled closer, kissing my cheek before resting his head on my shoulder. JT shot us a look of disgust. "You know you two are nauseatingly sweet together, don't you?"

We both grinned. I brought Tom's hand to my mouth and kissed his fingers. "Is that meant to be an insult? Because I take it as a compliment. It just shows how perfect we are together, doesn't it? Besides, you can't talk. I've seen you with Jules, and I've gotta tell you, you're just as bad."

JT rolled his eyes. "Not in the pub though. And not on quiz night. You two better not be so busy sucking each other's faces that you don't listen to the questions. I want to win tonight."

Tom leaned forward, exaggerating his careful scrutiny of my friend.

JT reared back, staring at him suspiciously. "What are you doing?"

"Committing that expression to memory so that when I paint you, I can get it right."

He stood up in a huff. "You're not painting me." He turned his attention to me. "Don't let him paint me."

I held my arms out in an expansive shrug. "Nothing to do with me. He can paint whatever he wants. I'm not the keeper of his brush." It was a running joke that Tom intended to paint JT, and it never failed to get a rise out of him. I had no idea why my big burly friend was so scared of being immortalized on canvas, but winding him up never got old.

JT made a noise of disgust. "I'm going for a smoke before the quiz starts." He waved a finger in our direction. "You can get your face sucking and your whispering sweet nothings to each other done while I'm gone."

We both waited until he'd disappeared from sight before bursting into laughter.

It had been three months since Tom's appearance on Christmas Day. There'd been no taking anything slowly. Once we'd released all the pent-up emotion of three years of separation in bed and uttered words of love several times over, there hadn't seemed much point in slow. Tom had left the hotel and moved in the next day, and had been there ever since. With no studio for him to paint in, we were looking for a place together, somewhere bigger but still close enough to my work. It just needed to have a spare room with enough light for a talented artist to create magic in. We'd had no luck so far but it was only a matter of time before something came up.

The initial meeting between Annabelle and Tom had been strained, to say the least. Just because I understood Tom's absence didn't mean she did, or was even prepared to try. Eventually, though—and it had taken over a month—she'd come to realize that he wasn't going anywhere. Now, there was a sort of grudging acceptance. I was hopeful that by the following Christmas, all the remaining wrinkles would have been ironed out of their relationship. Or at least enough that we could all sit down together for Christmas dinner without sly digs and sideways glances being the order of the day.

Tom hadn't been anywhere near Richmond. As far as his parents were concerned, he was still in Scotland, and that was the way he was happy to keep it. Given the new inner peace he projected, I was inclined to agree. He'd moved on. Tom didn't need any reminders of the way his life used to be. He was happier without his parents in his life, so why rock the boat. I did wonder though how long it would be before their paths crossed. But then, London was a huge city with millions of people in it, so perhaps they never would.

He'd sold three paintings so far, supplementing that income with a part-time job in an art gallery. I had every confidence that they would be the first of many. He had a bright future. I knew he did. There'd be more sales. And one day a gallery show to display his work. Tom laughed every time I told him that, but I was quietly confident. He was far too talented for someone not to spot his potential eventually.

Tom leaned in close, his lips hovering close to my ear. "Fancy a trip down Memory Lane?" When my brow furrowed and I didn't immediately pick up on what he was inferring, he inclined his head toward the pub bathroom and winked.

My cock immediately said yes, please. "We can't."

He raised an eyebrow. "Why not?"

"Well, for one, JT will kill us if we miss the start of the quiz."

Tom stood, turning to lean over me, a seductive smile on his face. "So we won't miss the start of the quiz. We'll be quick."

Indecision warred within me, just as it had years ago.

Tom leaned closer still, lowering his voice to a husky whisper. "I want to suck your cock. Come with me."

He held his hand out and I smiled and took it, following him through the same door where it had all begun. Where, although neither of us had realized it at the time, the first seeds of love had been sown and I'd been given riches for Christmas the likes of which I could never have dreamed of.

If you enjoyed this book, you might be interested in my upcoming fake relationship novella, Eager For You , available for pre-order on Amazon.

. . ⌘ . .

WHO BETTER TO FAKE it than two people who do it for a living?

Student Josh Keating, better known in the adult film world as Angel, has a problem. His family expect to meet his boyfriend that weekend. Except he doesn't have one. When fresh-faced newbie Leo Stone offers himself up to play the part, Josh finds it impossible to turn him down.

Damian Price's time as Leo Stone has only been a couple of months so far. His decision to join the studio heavily influenced by the huge torch he carries for Angel. He might just be his biggest fan. So of course, he's going to jump at the chance to play boyfriend for the weekend. As long as Josh doesn't get wind of Damian's true feelings or see through the little white lies he's been telling, everything will be fine.

One weekend.

One bed.

A growing mutual attraction.

An adult film star who's not above using his own performances for the purposes of seduction.

Can a fake relationship turn into a real one? Damian's keeping his fingers crossed it will.

Estimated release date December 16th 2019 Pre-order from Amazon[1]

. . ⌘ . .

SIGN UP TO MY NEWSLETTER to access a free 15k standalone story The Second Act as well as bonus chapters for my Too Far series and Edge of Living. Sign up through my website or at the following link. Download links are in the Welcome e-mail received after sign-up.

newsletter sign up[2]

. . ⌘ . .

---

1. http://getbook.at/Angel_HL_Day

2. http://eepurl.com/dw-7nH

THE SECOND ACT

Emerson White's on the verge of hitting the big time with his film career. After years of keeping his sexuality secret, he's just come out. Now his publicist is on his back demanding he take a respectable date to the film premiere. A man he's never met before. He's an actor though. How hard can it be to fake it for one night?

Except who should stroll in but Brent Walker, the love of Emerson's life. The man who walked out on him five years ago and didn't look back. Despite the painful memories, the chemistry between them hasn't faded one little bit.

One thing's for sure, it's going to be one hell of an evening. An evening they're unlikely to get through without raking up the past.

Is fake about to become real once more?

Thanks, from H.L Day

Thank you so much for choosing to read this book. You've made me really happy. How could you make me even happier? Well, you could leave a review. Then, I'd be ecstatic. :)

About H.L Day

H.L Day grew up in the North of England. As a child she was an avid reader, spending lots of time at the local library or escaping into the imaginary worlds created by the books she read. Her grandmother first introduced her to the genre of romance novels, as a teenager, and all the steamy sex they entailed. Naughty Grandma!

One day, H.L Day stumbled upon the world of m/m romance. She remained content to read other people's books for a while, before deciding to give it a go herself.

Now, she's a teacher by day and a writer by night. Actually, that's not quite true—she's a teacher by day, procrastinates about writing at night and writes in the school holidays, when she's not continuing to procrastinate. After all, there's books to read, places to go, people to see, exercise at the gym to do, films to watch. So many things to do—so few hours to do it in. Every now and again, she musters enough self-discipline to actually get some words onto paper—sometimes they even make sense and are in the right order.

Finding H.L Day

Where am I? I often ask myself the same question.

You can find me on Twitter[1].

You can find me on Instagram[2]

You can find me on Facebook.[3]

Send me a friend request or come and join my group -Days Den[4] for the most up to date information and for the chance at receiving ARCs

You can find me on my Website[5]

Or you can sign up to my newsletter[6] for new release updates.

1. https://twitter.com/HLDAY100

2. https://www.instagram.com/h.l.day101/?hl=en

3. https://www.facebook.com/profile.php?id=100010513175490

4. https://www.facebook.com/groups/2214565008830022/?ref=bookmarks

5. https://hldayauthor.co.uk/

6. https://wordpress.us18.list-manage.com/sub-scribe?u=e4815ef5cc09451a6bcd7aaa4&id=1875e83c44

More books from H.L Day

Temporary Situation (Temporary; Tristan and Dom #1)

A Personal assistant Dominic is a consummate professional. Funny then, that he harbors such unprofessional feelings toward Tristan Maxwell, the CEO of the company. No, not in that way. The man may be the walking epitome of gorgeousness dressed up in a designer suit. But, Dominic's immune. Unlike most of the workforce, he can see through the pretty facade to the arrogant, self-entitled asshole below. It's lucky then, that the man's easy enough to avoid.

Disaster strikes when Dominic finds himself having to work in close proximity as Tristan's P.A. The man is infuriatingly unflappable, infuriatingly good-humored, and infuriatingly unorthodox. In short, just infuriating. A late-night rescue leading to a drunken pass only complicates matters further, especially with the discovery that Tristan is both straight and engaged.

Hatred turns to tolerance, tolerance to friendship, and friendship to mutual passion. One thing's for sure, if Tristan sets his sights on Dominic, there's no way Dominic has the necessary armor or willpower to keep a force of nature like Tristan at bay for long, no matter how unprofessional a relationship with the boss might be. He may just have to revise everything he previously thought and believed in for a chance at love.

Buy now from Amazon[1]

A Christmas Situation (Temporary; Tristan and Dom #1.5)

Love conquers all. But can it survive Christmas?

Dominic and Tristan have been together for almost a year. So everything's got to be plain sailing, right? Not quite. Not if you ask Dominic. Tristan's a bundle of energy and crazy ideas at the best of times. Add in Christmas, and it's a recipe for disaster.

That's not the only issue. There's also Tristan's mysterious absences and secret phone calls to contend with. Dominic might be insecure, but he's not crazy. His boyfriend is definitely up to something, and neither family nor friends seem interested in listening to his concerns. He won't jump to conclusions this time though. He'll talk to Tristan. Only what do you do when you can't get a straight answer out of the man you love?

When Tristan's secrets are revealed, will their first Christmas together also be their last? Or is Dominic about to discover that all his worries have been for nothing?

Only time will tell.

A story containing Christmas snark; a drunk Tristan; snow; and absolutely no mention of spiders—well alright, maybe a few mentions.

Buy from Amazon[2]

---

2.   http://getbook.at/ACS

Temporary Insanity (Temporary; Paul and Indy #1)

Sleeping with the enemy never felt so good.

When Paul Davenport comes face to face with the man he caught in bed with his boyfriend years before, it's hate at first sight. Well, second sight. Indy should be apologizing, not flirting. Except the gorgeous barman is completely oblivious to their paths ever having crossed before.

Despite his feelings, Paul's powerless to resist the full-on charm offensive that follows. It's fine though. It's just sex. No emotions. No getting to know each other. Just a bout of temporary insanity that's sure to run its course once the simmering passion starts to wear off.

Only what if it's not? Indy's nothing like the man Paul expected him to be from his past actions. What if they're perfect for each other and Paul's just too stubborn to see it? Forging a relationship with him would require an emotional U-turn Paul might not be capable of making.

There's a thin line between love and hate, and Paul's about to discover just how thin it really is. He can't possibly be falling for the man that ruined his life. Can he?

Warning: This book contains hate sex—sort of, lots of banter, and a pink elephant. No, really it does. Actually, two elephants.

Please note: Although this book is in the Temporary series, it occurs during the same timeline as A Temporary Situation. Therefore, both books can be read as standalones and in any order.

Buy from Amazon[3]

Time for a Change

What if the last thing you want, might be the very thing you need?

Stuffy and uptight accountant Michael's life is exactly the way he likes it: ordered, routine and risk-free. He doesn't need chaos and he doesn't need anything shaking it up and causing him anxiety. The only blot on the horizon is the small matter of getting his ex-boyfriend Christian back. That's exactly the type of man Michael goes for: cultured, suave and sophisticated.

Coffee shop employee Sam is none of those things. He's a ball of energy and happiness who thinks nothing of flaunting his half-naked muscular body and devastating smile in front of Michael when he's trying to work. He knows what he wants—and that's Michael. And no matter how much Michael tries to resist him, he's not going to take no for an answer.

Sam eventually chips through Michael's barriers and straight into his bed. But Michael's already made some questionable decisions that might just come back to haunt him. He's got some difficult choices to make if he's ever going to find love. And he might just find that he's too set in his ways to make the right ones quickly enough. If Michael's not careful, the best thing that's ever happened to him might just slip right through his fingers. Because even a patient man like Sam has his limits.

Buy from Amazon[4]

Kept in the Dark

Struggling actor Dean only escorts occasionally to pay the bills. So, his first instinct on being offered a job with a strange set of conditions is to turn it down. No date. Don't switch the lights on. Don't touch him. I mean, what's that all about? What's the man trying to hide? Dean certainly doesn't expect sex with a faceless stranger to spark so much passion inside him. It's just business though, right? He can put a stop to it whenever he wants.

When Dean meets Justin—a scarred, ex-army soldier unlucky in love. Dean's given a chance at a proper relationship. He can see past the scars to the man underneath. He's everything Dean could possibly wish for in a boyfriend: kind, caring and sweet. All Dean needs to do is be honest. Easy, right? But, Justin's holding back and Dean can't work out why. But whatever it is, it's enough to give him second thoughts.

They both have secrets which could shatter their fledgling relationship. After all, secrets have a nasty habit of coming out eventually. The question is when they do, will they be able to piece their relationship back together? Or will they be left with nothing but memories of bad decisions and the promise of the love they could have had, if only they'd both been honest and fought harder.

Buy from Amazon[5]

Also available in audio

---

5.   http://getbook.at/KITD

Refuge (Fight for Survival #1)

If you no longer recognise someone, how can you possibly be expected to trust them with your life?

Some might describe Blake Brannigan's life in the small Yorkshire village of Thwaite as bordering on mundane. His job in a café doesn't exactly set the world alight. But, he's got his own house, a boyfriend, and a close-knit group of good friends. For him, that's more than enough to lead a contented life.

Then in one fell swoop, everything's ripped away when he's forced to flee the village with only his boyfriend for company. He doesn't know why they're leaving. He hasn't got the faintest clue what's going on, and he's struggling to understand the actions and behaviour of a man he thought he knew. A man that it soon becomes clear knows far more about what's happening than he's letting on. A man hiding a multitude of secrets.

When the true extent of what's happening comes to light, Blake is rocked to the core. Peril lurks around every corner. The smallest decision suddenly spells the difference between life and death. If Blake's to have any chance of survival in this new and frightening world, he's going to have to unearth buried secrets, figure out whether love really can conquer all, and face emotional, physical, and mental challenges the likes of which he could never have imagined.

One thing's for sure, when life suddenly boils down to nothing more than the desperate need to find refuge, priorities change. Blake's certainly have.

Buy from Amazon[6]

---

6.   http://mybook.to/Refugebk1

Taking Love's Lead

Zachary Cole's new personal shopper is stunning in more ways than one. Gone is the staid, professional Jonathan. In his place is sexy, whirlwind Edgar, whose methods and lifestyle are less than orthodox. Still reeling from the experience, Zack can't get him out of his head. He needs to see him again. Even if it does involve dragging his heavily pregnant sister and her dalmatian into his cunning plan.

Sick of being dumped yet again, dog walker Edgar's pledged to stay single and put energy into finding a career more suited to an adult instead. Zack might be extremely tempting...and just happen to pop up wherever he goes, but that doesn't mean he's going to change his mind. He's got bigger priorities in life than a website designer who's after a brief walk on the wild side. Edgar's heart has taken enough of a bruising. He's not prepared to get dumped again.

Zack wants love. Edgar only wants friendship. Can the two men find common ground amid the chaos of Edgar's life? Or is Zack going to find that no matter what he does, there's no happy ending and he'll have to walk away?

Warning: This story contains dogs. Lots of dogs. Big ones. Small ones. Naughty ones. Ones that like ducks, squirrels, and lakes and ones that like to be carried. No dogs were harmed in the writing of this book.

Buy from Amazon[7]

---

7.   http://getbook.at/TheZon

Edge of Living

Sometimes, death can feel like the only escape.

It's been a year since Alex stopped living. He exists. He breathes. He pretends to be like everyone else. But, he doesn't live. Burdened by memories, he dreams of the day when he can finally be free. Until that time comes, he keeps everybody at bay. It's been easy so far. But he never factored in meeting a man like Austin.

Hard-working mechanic Austin has always gone for men as muscular as himself. So, it's a mystery why he's so bewitched by the slim, quiet man with the soulful brown eyes who works in the library. The magnetic attraction is one thing, but the protective instincts are harder to fathom. Austin's sure, though, that if he can only earn Alex's trust, then the two of them could be perfect together.

A tentative relationship begins. But Alex's secrets run deep. Far deeper than Austin could ever envisage. Time is ticking. Events are coming to a head, and love is never a magic cure. Oblivious to the extent of Alex's pain, can Austin discover the truth? Or is he destined to be left alone, only able to piece together the fragments of his boyfriend's history, once it's already too late?

Trigger warning: Please be aware that this story deals with suicidal ideation and other dark themes. If this is a subject you find uncomfortable, then this book is not recommended.

Despite this, there is a guaranteed HEA.

Buy from Amazon[8]

---

8. http://mybook.to/EdgeofLiving

A Dance too Far (Too Far #1)

Love can be dangerous!

Valentin Bychkov, rising star of contemporary Russian ballet, appears to have everything: wealth, talent, success, and a face and body to match. Not that anyone can get close. Bypass the entourage and there's still Valentin's sharp tongue and acerbic wit to deal with. He may give his body freely, but his emotions are kept tightly locked away.

Max Farley's life is a simple one. All he's interested in is work, drinking, and picking up the latest in a long line of one-night stands. The way he chooses to live may not be to everyone's taste but it suits him down to the ground. He's never met anyone who's made him want to confront the demons from his past. Until now.

A show in London brings the two together. Lust brings them closer still. But if rumors of Bratva connections turn out to be true, then dangerous men wait in the wings. One dangerous man in particular, who's used to people following his orders without question.

Difficult choices need to be made on both sides. Valentin and Max need to stop playing with fire and let each other go, or face the consequences. But letting go isn't that easy where love is concerned.

And some things are worth the risk.

Warning: This book contains a snarky ballet dancer with an aversion to clothes, a little too much wall sex and an overabundance of Russian heavies.

Buy now from Amazon[9]

Coming to audio in December 2019

---

9.   http://mybook.to/ADancetooFar

A Step too Far (Too Far #2)

Two men. Three identities. An unstoppable attraction.

Desperate for his luck to change, Jake Spencer manages to land a dance contract with Dmitry Gruzdev. The job has plenty of perks, including a simmering lust between him and Dmitry's hulking brute of a bodyguard, Mikhail. Life is finally looking up. Except as the shine wears off, it becomes clear that Jake's stepped into a world of darkness and depravity where Bratva answers to no one and allies are not what they seem.

Mikhail's hiding a secret: there is no Mikhail. He's simply a front for undercover operative, Ryan Harris. A means to gain access to Dmitry. Ryan's not stupid. There's no way he's going to get distracted by a pretty face, no matter how attractive Jake might be. That would be far too dangerous for all concerned. Only it's not that simple and before Ryan knows it, the line between personal and professional begins to blur spectacularly.

Lust develops into more. Secrets start to unravel. Ryan's got an impossible choice to make: keep Jake safe or maintain his cover. But how much does Dmitry know? The hunted may be about to become the hunter, blowing both men's worlds to pieces and leaving them with nothing.

Can a relationship built on lies ever lead to love?

Warning: This book contains a seductive dancer prone to getting into trouble, a gruff man who's anything but, and a villain who just won't go away.

Buy now from Amazon[10]

Coming to Audio in January 2020

---

10.   http://getbook.at/A Step too Far

Printed in Great Britain
by Amazon

12325106R00081